DRUNK BEFORE DAWN

To Bill, Heather and Val, without
whom this book would never have
seen the light of day.

Shirley Lees

DRUNK BEFORE DAWN

OMF BOOKS

© Overseas Missionary Fellowship

First published . . . . April 1979

ISBN 0 85363 128 X

*Illustrations by Jan Detterman,
cover and maps by Val Kay*

*Made in Great Britain
Published by Overseas Missionary Fellowship,
Belmont, The Vine, SEVENOAKS, Kent, TN13 3TZ
and printed at The Camelot Press Ltd, Southampton*

CONTENTS

Part 4

A new dawn   1970–1978

Maps can be found on pages 12, 22, 70, 88 and 172

SOME SIGNIFICANT DATES

1st September	1928	Inaugural meeting of BEM
12th November	1928	Arrival Kuching
June/August	1933	First visits to Trusan
13th November	1937	Day of Prayer
21st November	1937	Permission to enter Trusan
17th December	1941	Japanese land in Miri
27th April	1945	Death of Frank Davidson
August/Sept	1946	Missionaries return
5th May	1947	Opening of Lawas Bible school
5th June	1947	Long Tebangan 'turning'
23rd June	1950	Slamat lands at Lawas
14–25 August	1950	BEM adopts fifteen-year policy
8th June	1951	First interior landing, Long Atip
7–12 December	1959	Formation of the SIB
6th May	1962	Lun Bawang New Testament presented to SIB
31st August	1963	Malaysia Day
17th June	1969	BEM to Kuching
August	1972	Miri Bible College established
11–15 December	1972	Peterus Octavianus at SIB Conference
October	1973	Revival, Bario
February	1974	SIB broadcasting over FEBC
17th November	1974	SIB church at Kota Kinabalu
28th March	1974	Merger between BEM and OMF
January/March	1975	Administration moves to Miri
6–10 December	1976	SIB Sabah constituted
January	1978	First East Malaysians on staffs of MBC and the Advanced Bible School, Lawas

FOREWORD

THIS is the wonderful story of God at work in one of the most fascinating parts of the world I have had the privilege of visiting. My wife and I were thrilled by all that we experienced in three short weeks in 1975, but the writer of this book was no mere visitor to Borneo. She can write about so much firsthand, having worked in Borneo for fourteen years with her doctor husband among the Tagal people in Sabah, where also two of her daughters were born.

It is moving to see thriving churches that have come into existence within one's own lifetime, and though I knew some of this history before, I have found myself stirred afresh by reading this epic story. We are all delighted when we see one friend or neighbour come to Christ, but in Borneo it is first whole families converted, and then whole longhouses transformed and then whole tribes with a new lifestyle. In recent years Western Christians have been interested in living in community, but nowhere else have I seen seven hundred Christians living under one longhouse roof, rarely experienced so genuine a welcome nor what seemed an almost idyllic way of life importing very little from outside the jungle world. We never saw the contrast with what they were before Christ lifted them to newness of life, but I chuckled at the story of the visiting curator of the Sarawak museum. He had seen the desperate condition of the tribe on an earlier visit and thought them past redemption: now, astonished at the transformation, he exclaims, 'What on earth have you done to these people, Southwell?'

This book gives a realistic picture of tribal missionary

work in a developing country, still without roads in the interior. I was filled with admiration for all the early missionaries endured. The swollen mountain streams with dangerous rapids, the lowland jungle swamps to be crossed, the primitive living conditions where first snakes and then the jungle take over your home if you leave it empty for a while. They had to put up with irregular mail, shortage of funds and internment by the Japanese. They faced the hostility and then the mixed motives of the tribes towards their message. The government was at times reluctant to allow them into the interior at all, content rather to let certain tribes die out because they were rotten with alcoholism and disease. And on top of all this the supreme problem of communicating their message intelligibly across multiple language barriers – 'no dictionary, of course, no written language, no teachers and no linguistic training'.

There are highlights to remember – Winsome Southwell hiding a precious translated manuscript of Mark's Gospel on a washing line in internment camp to keep it from the Japanese; Ray Cunningham, desperately sick with typhoid miles from anywhere, struggling down to where he could put through a call for help by radio, and being rescued by one of the courageous pilots who pioneered aviation in Borneo; Frank Davidson, who died in internment, remembered by his wife Enid 'sitting at his desk at 5 o'clock each morning, reading by the light of his [paraffin] hunting lamp, deep in prayer as he sought God's will for the day and His enabling power' – seeking to follow the example of Him who said 'I delight to do Thy will, O my God'.

Most of all there is praise to the God who does such wonders – sustaining the missionaries in all their journeyings and agonizings, working wonderfully in the hearts of the headhunting tribesmen, transforming them into men and women of God, giving them the desire to see new congregations planted and perfected – and most of all to read of the Lord's work in convicting His people of sin during the revival brings the greatest blessings to our own hearts.

Read on then: you are in for a treat. But do not forget to go on praying for these churches and their leaders as they wrestle with the new problems created for the newly-educated young people moving down to the coastal towns for more lucrative jobs. And most of all to pray for those still unreached, especially the vast majority of the Iban of Sarawak, the largest of the tribes, who said – 'We will believe some day'.

Michael Griffiths
General Director,
Overseas Missionary
Fellowship

EAST MALAYSIA

COUNTRY BORDERS
DIVISION BOUNDARIES

SCALE IN MILES

0   50   100

SABAH

KAJAU
DUSUN
KOTA BELUD
DUSUN • MT. KINABALU
KOTA • RANAU
KINABALU • TAMBUNAN
PADAS R. & BEAUFORT
TENOM
WESTON
BRUNEI BAY
LABUAN
TAGAL
LAWAS
LUN DAWANG
LIMBANG
BISAYA FIFTH DIVISION
BRUNEI
KELABIT HIGHLANDS
KAYAN SABAH
PENAN KENAH
BARAM R.
MIRI KENYA
FOURTH DIVISION
IBAN
BINTULU KENYA
IBAN
BERAWAN
BELAGA
BEKETAN
PUNAN BA IBAN
SEVENTH DIVISION
MELANAU REJANG R.
THIRD DIVISION
SIBU
IBAN
SIXTH DIVISION
IBAN
SECOND DIVISION

KUCHING
FIRST DIVISION LAND DAYAK

KALIMANTAN

MALAYA
MALAYSIA SABAH
SUMATRA KALIMANTAN
JAVA CELEBES
AUSTRALIA

PREFACE

Dawn over the longhouses of the interior hills of Borneo frequently revealed drunken forms lying in abandoned postures all over the floor. Others would still be drinking from the huge jars of potent rice beer, and the feasts would continue for several days. The Lun Bawang people were particularly given to such drunken orgies. They were the most despised people of Borneo and they were dying out. But a breathtaking new dawn broke for them between 1933 and 1938, when God stepped in to build the Church among them. He so transformed them that soon their neighbours the Kelabits, and after them men and women from many other tribes, were asking how they too could follow this new way. The church was beginning to grow.

In the last few years there has been yet another new dawn for that Church, reminding many of the second chapter of Acts.

'How can we be drunk, when it is only 9 a.m.?' Peter asked when the disciples were accused of being drunk at Pentecost. He explained what had happened with reference to the book of Joel:

'I will pour out my Spirit on all people.
Your sons and daughters will prophesy,
Your young men will see visions
And your old men will dream dreams.
Even on my servants both men and women,
I will pour out my Spirit in those days and they will
    prophesy.'   (NIV)

Starting in the Kelabit Highlands, this has been happening in many parts of Borneo as God has intervened yet again in the further building of His Church.

Buildings usually need scaffolding and although God has at times worked in these sovereign and spectacular ways, He also called together a team of missionaries to be used as the scaffolding for the building of this part of His Church. The first three young men of the Borneo Evangelical Mission arrived in Borneo in 1928. Since then, God has called many more men and women from different countries and backgrounds. Through them He has established the Sidang Injil Borneo (the Evangelical Church in Borneo) and He is now using them to assist the SIB pastors and teachers in the continued building up of that Church.

This is the story of how God has formed a Church in Borneo from the raw material of drunken tribesmen. It is written, not to bring honour to the scaffolding nor indeed to the building, but to bring glory to the Architect and Builder.

CHAPTER 1

COURT CASES CANCELLED

'**D**IFFERENT' was the word that occurred over and over again as I sat on a patterned reed mat on the floor, chatting to the Penghulu (native chief) of the Kelabit Highlands of East Malaysia.

'It is so different in my family now', he commented as he looked across at his beautiful though slightly ageing little wife. She smiled agreement as she squatted quietly and serenely, pouring out cups of weak, sweet black coffee for the visitors.

The Kelabit Highlands are rugged and remote. Prior to the building of the first little airstrip in 1953 they were almost inaccessible. The people were left to themselves by all but a rare Government officer whose duty took him there, and one or two dedicated missionaries who faced several weeks of arduous walking, climbing and wading of fast-flowing rivers to visit their villages.

But change came quickly once it had begun and the Penghulu's life has spanned that change. Born into an illiterate spirit-fearing community, he had seen over twenty Kelabits enter University by 1976, thirty years after the establishment of the first primary school.

Guru Paul, a vivacious little Timorese pastor from Indonesia, had founded that school in 1946, and taught his Christian faith to the Kelabits. He had married a Kelabit and sitting with us on this occasion was his second son, Elisa, who had just returned from All Nations Christian College in England. He was soon to become the first Bornean member of staff of the Miri Bible College.

The Penghulu himself was trained as an upriver medical assistant or 'dresser' before being chosen to lead his people, but he had sometimes been doubtful whether his promotion was worthwhile.

'I used to long to change my well-paid job as Penghulu for my former job as dresser', he explained to me. 'The pay was much smaller but the job much less tiring. As Penghulu I never stopped. I was always being called here and there to arbitrate in disputes. I was so tired. Many nights I would not get to sleep until the early hours of the morning as the arguments went on and on.'

'How are things so different now?' I asked.

'The revival has changed everything. I have hardly any disputes to settle now. When my people have an argument or dispute, they get together, discuss and pray together and settle the matter. They don't need to call me to arbitrate any more.'

This seemed a rather sweeping statement, but he continued to verify it.

'Even the District Officer asked me how it was that my file was so empty, when it used to be as full as those of the other Penghulus. I had one court case in 1974, two in 1975 and still only three last year. I told the DO that it was because the Holy Spirit had come in blessing to our villages.'

I had certainly noticed that attitudes were very different. The church services, including the pre-dawn prayer meeting every morning, were alive and well attended and it was now four years since the revival. I pressed the Penghulu to tell me more.

'When the revival started we didn't think it could be from God because it was just the young people who had been blessed. Some of us in fact thought they were mad. I carefully avoided them at first because I was afraid they would tell me I was wicked. But then I began to see the change in their lives. The Bible says, "If you seek you will find", and so I urgently began to seek whatever it was that had made so much difference to these young people.'

With the understandable exaggeration of one who had experienced an exciting new dimension to his Christian faith, he continued as though his people had not really experienced any change in their lives from becoming Christians.

'The whole economy of our house is different now', he said. 'Look at my wife and children. They can wear nice *bajus* and *sarongs* now [Bornean type blouse and skirt]. I don't waste all my money any more. When you smoke and drink as we Kelabits used to, you have to spend a lot of money. Your wife and children don't have enough to eat. Then they get tempted to steal.'

I looked around the room where we were sitting. It was obviously the room of someone whose life had been affected by a meaningful Christian experience for many years. It was spacious, well kept, clean. Outside I had noticed that the neatly handsawn and planed boards had been painted and the grounds surrounding the whole longhouse were immaculately clean. It was so different from the pagan longhouses that I had visited many years before, and indeed those I visited on this return trip to Borneo at the end of 1977.

It had been built long before the revival, during the sixties, when the Government had encouraged them and others to move onto the Bario plain. Confrontation between Indonesia and Malaysia had made the border country a danger zone. They had selected the present site, a small hill overlooking the wet rice fields of the plain. It had been quite a job taking off the top of the hill. They had hoes, one or two wheelbarrows and some makeshift trays from the ends of oil drums. The Kelabits are never lacking in ingenuity and the flotsam of war had come in very useful. They are also vigorous and hard working and they had taken off a great deal of soil, but still there was not enough space for all the family rooms to be built traditionally into one long straight house. They had decided to build it in an L-shape. But it was well built and demonstrated clearly the changes which had taken place when the whole tribe had turned to Christianity during the forties.

I climbed down the hill and crossed through the rich green rice fields to Bario, the longhouse from which the plain takes its name. This was the former Penghulu's house. It was somewhat longer and built on the conveniently levelled ground of the original little airstrip which the Kelabits themselves had built to open up this very remote and isolated part of the country. The airstrip had been made obsolete by the wider and longer Government strip built at the opposite end of the plain.

I and my companions climbed the notched log into the room of the late Penghulu's son-in-law, Ulit Matu. My husband and I had met him many years before when he and his fellow Kelabit deacons had walked for many days, because of their hunger to be taught the Word of God. He is a flamboyant, exuberant character and greeted me like a long-lost friend.

'You remember me, don't you?' he asked in his booming voice and laughed heartily when I had to admit that I had forgotten his name.

He and his wife laid out mats for us, kindly placing them by the low wall so that we could have the comfort of support for our backs. They then sat with their backs to the central fireplace. For an hour or two they sat bolt upright with no support as only those can who have been sitting on the floor all their lives.

'People say it is the young people who have changed', Ulit Matu began. 'But we old folk have changed too. We used to have the skin of Christians. But now it is something inside. Everything is so different now.'

Again there was the word 'different', and the feeling that the revival had so changed their lives that they wondered whether they had even been Christians before. But

18

undoubtedly they had. Ulit Matu himself had been one of the first Kelabits to take the great step of faith over thirty years ago. They had defied the evil spirits and turned from the absolute fear and bondage of their animistic beliefs to the freedom which Christ gave. But he and many others had hung on to what he called the 'social customs associated with our former beliefs'. Many of them had continued in the excessive (though somewhat moderated) drinking and smoking for which most of the interior tribes of Borneo were renowned. But nevertheless the change to the Christian faith had been very real and had profoundly affected their whole livelihood. Robert Lian Saging, one of the first Kelabits to graduate, points this out in his honours degree thesis at Kuala Lumpur University:

'The greatest thing to have happened in the history of the Kelabit people was the conversion of the tribe to Christianity. The developments in the Kelabit country carried out by the Government in the last thirty years have been a success mainly because of the effect of Christianity on the Kelabits. Christianity has played, is still playing and will continue to play a leading role in the lives and developments of the Kelabit tribe. The Kelabit church is the power and strength of the Kelabit people. The main effect that Christianity has had on the Kelabits is the change of the Kelabit society from a pagan and unprogressive one to a Christian and progressive one.'[1]

Progressive they certainly are. The first Kelabit doctor has recently qualified. Others are in universities or other forms of training while already many have well-paid jobs in coastal towns. The Highlands too have altered, with an almost-daily air service flying goods and people in and out of Bario. The standard of living has improved and illiteracy among the young is a thing of the past.

Christian they certainly are too. The vision of an

[1] Robert Lian Saging: 'An Ethno-History of the Kelabit Tribe of Sarawak', 1976/7 Honours Degree Thesis at Kuala Lumpur University.

established, indigenous church which inspired the three pioneers of the BEM has come to fruition, not only among the Kelabits but among many other interior tribes. As I flew out of Bario, I looked down at those seemingly endless green mountains over which the pioneers had climbed, and I mused how good it would have been if they had all lived to see this day.

PART 1

JUST BEFORE THE DAWN

1928 – 1938

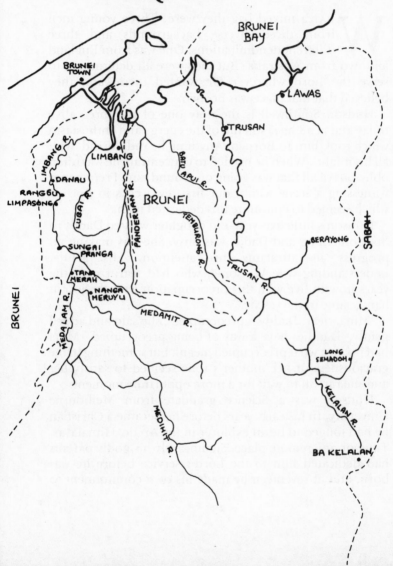

LIMBANG RIVER AREA

BRUNEI BAY

BRUNEI TOWN

LAWAS

TRUSAN

LIMBANG

LIMBANG R.

DANAU

RANGGU
LIMPASONG

LUBAI R.

BRUNEI

BATU APUI R.

PANDERUAN R.

TEMBURONG R.

BERAYONG

SUNGAI
PRANGA

TRUSAN R.

SABAH

TANA
MERAH

NANGA
MERUYU

MEDALAM R.

MEDAMIT R.

BRUNEI

LONG
SEMADOH

KELALAN R.

MEDIHIT R.

BA KELALAN

CHAPTER 2

NOT ANOTHER MISSION!

W HAT a mixed bag they were! Three young men from three diverse backgrounds and three different denominations. One was from England and two from Australia. But they were all determined to serve the Lord wherever He wanted them, and they believed that that place was Borneo.

Hudson Southwell is the only one of the three alive today and at 78 he is still full of the energy and enthusiasm which took him to Borneo. Anything he did, he did 'with all his might'. When he needed to concentrate he was often oblivious of all that was going on around him. I remember witnessing a scene within our first few weeks in Borneo which seemed to epitomize this dedicated man.

Hudson's little five-year-old daughter wanted Daddy to 'fix' something and Daddy was busy. She was making no progress in attracting his attention. His gentle, understanding wife Winsome, who had learnt over the years how to live with this preoccupation with the job in hand, came to the rescue.

'Mina, dear, Daddy is preoccupied', she said and added gently, 'Daddies have a way of being preoccupied.' Mina had no idea what preoccupied meant, but something in the graciousness of her mother's tone seemed to satisfy her and she ran off to wait for a more opportune moment.

Hudson was a Science graduate from Melbourne University. In his early years before he became a Christian he had longed to be an explorer in the Arctic, Himalayas, Tibet or any remote place. Significantly his godly parents had dedicated him to the Lord's service before he was born, and at seventeen he made his own commitment to missionary service, if God wanted to use his 'itchy feet'. But this was shortly after he had been given a student teaching scholarship which meant that he was bonded for nine years, five of training and then four in technical education. Missionary friends wisely advised him not to try to get release from his bond, and so it was not until he was 26 that he went to the Melbourne Bible Institute to prepare himself for whatever the Lord had in mind for him.

It was here that he met Frank Davidson and Carey Tolley. Frank was interested in everything, just like Hudson. He had been born in England, second son of the managing director of Morgan and Scott the publishers. The family had emigrated to Australia when Frank was sixteen. He was a tall, vigorous type of man, ideally suited to pioneering work, and might have been the Englishman's picture of the typical Australian. But he had had an English public school education and considered himself an Englishman. A close Australian friend described him as 'deliberately retaining the manners of a well-educated English gentleman who was critical of the casual manners of most Australians'.

Frank was obviously gifted with young people and he spent much of his vacations while at Melbourne Bible Institute on evangelistic tours in the East Gippsland area of Victoria. He shared these occasions with two young men who lived near the Davidsons' farm. Their aunt was one of the first members of the BEM Council and their sister later became Winsome Southwell.

Hudson and Frank were extroverts, good conversationalists owing to their wide interests in many spheres. They had strong and decided ideas and perhaps somewhat overshadowed the shy, quieter Carey Tolley. As Florence, his widow, pointed out, 'Carey was in some ways the "odd man out" of the three.' But he was no less a pioneer and was perhaps the most inveterate traveller of them all – no small achievement among three such dedicated and indomitable men.

The Principal of MBI, the Rev. C. H. Nash, described Carey as 'the man of prayer' and this seems to have been so. Hudson tells of the six foot by six foot leaf hut which Carey built for himself 20 yards or so away from the little house in which they all lived at their first base. It was a haven where he could get away on his own. There he could be quiet with the Lord and pray, particularly for those many tribal people whom he met and to whom he preached during his frequent travelling.

These three young men were in training at MBI because they had felt the call of God to overeas service. Mr Nash had been stirring the students to consider their responsibilities for the Southern Pacific, and the three were soon meeting together to pray for Borneo.

It was perhaps a little surprising that Hudson was not thinking of going to China, because all the formative influences in his missionary thinking up to that time had been missionaries from the China Inland Mission (now the Overseas Missionary Fellowship). Was he not called Hudson after the great founder of that Mission – Hudson Taylor whom his father had known when Hudson Taylor visited Australia in the 1890's? But the influence did not go unnoticed. The Mission which he helped to found was based firmly on the same principles and practices as the CIM, a factor which simplified the merger with OMF fifty years later.

With characteristic enthusiasm, as they met together to pray, Hudson started looking for books and especially maps of Borneo. All the maps he could find were of different scales, but he soon found a way of reducing them all to the same scale. Then he drew his own map on the largest piece of drawing paper he could find. This map hung on the wall of the BEM office in Melbourne until it was replaced many years later by the map made by Hudson during his hundreds of miles of travelling, using time lapse and compass bearings. This was the most detailed and accurate map of those parts until Confrontation justified the expense of aerial photography. Hudson was fascinated by maps.

'The first time I met Hudson', Winsome recalls, 'he was carrying a map of Borneo under his arm.'

That fascination with maps helped the young men to build a picture of the land to which they felt drawn, though not yet knowing whether this was God's call.

'Borneo became real', was Hudson's comment years later.

But how were they to know whether God wanted them there, and how were they to get there if He did? They turned to their Principal for advice.

Mr Nash had been trained at Ridley Hall, Cambridge and had founded the small Bible Training Institute in Melbourne in 1922. He had once thought that he was called to missionary service himself, but through the overruling wisdom of God he put his great missionary vision and insight into training young men and later young women, to go instead. By 1926 there were a hundred students enrolled at MBI and it was to become one of the largest Bible Institutes in Australia,

As the young men prayed and talked with Mr Nash, they reached the point in May 1928 when they felt they must 'seek a definite word from the Lord'. They had explored the possibilities of going out under the auspices of other missions. Each one in turn, however, had indicated that they could not consider starting up a new work in Sarawak. For some it was a time of retrenchment rather than advance. Naturally they approached the China Inland Mission. Recalling the request, the present OMF director, Michael Griffiths, noted with a smile in the light of the

26

recent merger, that Hudson Taylor's successor had said, 'The Lord has not led us beyond China'.

In view of this should they go out supporting themselves through their own efforts, as did Paul 'the tentmaker', or should they start a new mission with all the complications and uncertainties involved? It would have to be interdenominational as Hudson was a Baptist, Carey was Brethren and Frank was an Anglican. During these years of the Depression, where would they find people to support them if they went out alone?

With these thoughts in mind they separated 'to give themselves to prayer'. On 17th May they met again, each one coming with assurances from the Lord.

'The Lord gave me the verse in Philippians 4', Hudson explained. 'In everything, by prayer and supplication, with thanksgiving, let your requests be made known unto God. And the peace of God . . . shall keep you. . . .' All agreed that this should be their charter. They were to go out in faith, looking only to God and with thanksgiving, knowing His peace.

As further confirmation that a new mission should be formed, they received a letter that very afternoon (posted two days earlier in Queensland). It was from Stafford Young, a businessman from a wealthy family which was deeply involved in missions. In it he offered £50 for expenses for sending someone out to Borneo. It was a very substantial gift in those days and was taken to be the Lord's seal on the deliberations of that afternoon meeting at MBI.

Yet another indication that God was guiding was received after Frank had returned to his evangelistic work in Gippsland. The minister at a church service where Frank was preaching mentioned Frank's growing conviction that God wanted him in Borneo. Frank happened to make the comment that he had never met anyone who had been to Borneo, and a young lady in the congregation went home and told her landlord, a Mr Henderson.

Mr Henderson was a Christian who had been in Borneo as a trader for seven years. He therefore knew the area and spoke the language. On 23rd June 1928 a meeting was held with him in Yalloun and he offered his help. They then all returned to Melbourne for the weekend for further discussion. Mr Henderson agreed to accompany the three men to Borneo for a short period to help them make the initial contacts and settle in to the land and its ways.

Several informal meetings were held in the next weeks to discuss the formation of a Borneo Fellowship, and on 28th July 1928 the first formal statement was made.

'It was resolved to take steps for the formation of a Borneo Fellowship. Rev. C. H. Nash was asked to act as Chairman of the group, Mr C. H. Southwell to act as Honorary Secretary and Mr R. S. Tregaskis (Treasurer of MBI) as Honorary Treasurer. A statement for circulation was adopted, setting before the Christian public the present position.' This statement included the following summary of the position up to that point:

'For some time past the needs of Borneo's unevangelised millions have been laid on the hearts of some of the students at the MBI, and a little band has met to pray for the evangelisation of the untouched pagan tribes of Central Borneo.

'By a series of providential leadings, three men have come to the point of offering their lives for such service, and the time now appears ripe for the issue of a first statement to be put forth among the Lord's people in Australia in the confident belief that it is His good pleasure that preparations should be made for advance. The first requirement is Prayer. . . . It is felt that the time is ripe for a wider fellowship in prayer that God may make clear His will as to the next move, and that the way may speedily open up for a strong forward movement into Borneo. We therefore invite communications from those upon whose hearts this burden is laid, with a view to their incorporation in this Fellowship for Borneo.'

Further meetings were held, council members were appointed from many different denominations and the name Borneo Evangelical Mission was adopted on 31st August. The inaugural meeting was arranged for 1st September when the final draft of the constitution was prepared and agreed to. This was to be ratified at the next Council meeting.

The Borneo Evangelical Mission had been born.

Iban boy learning to smoke

CHAPTER 3

SMALL BEGINNINGS

THE s.s. *Newby Hall* sailed from Melbourne on 5th October 1928, carrying the three young men who were going out to an almost totally unknown situation. They knew they would have to learn by experience and maybe by their mistakes. With them was the retired Mr. Henderson who was accompanying them for an initial period only, and then they would be totally on their own. But they were all assured that God had called them.

After a warm welcome from the Secretary of the Bible Society in Singapore, Mr. Henderson and Hudson Southwell set off for Kuching, leaving Carey Tolley and Frank Davidson to wait in Singapore for news of permission to work in Sarawak.

Sailing up the Sarawak river, they arrived at the tiny, sprawling capital on 12th November 1928. On the opposite bank, surrounded by green lawns and shady trees, stood a strange mixture of medieval castle and modern tropical bungalow. It was the palace of the White Rajahs who had been exercising their firm but benevolent rule for more than three-quarters of a century.

The two men were received with considerable suspicion at first, not even being allowed to stay off the boat for three days. But eventually their request was given a favourable hearing. Other missions were already working in many of the more populated areas and the Government had a strict zoning policy which they maintained for many years to come. They felt it wise to keep the various missionary groups as widely separated as possible. No one was working in the Limbang area in the north, nor around

Bintulu in the central coastal area, so the newcomers were given a choice. After careful consideration, it was decided that they should go to the Limbang area in the Fifth Division.

Sarawak was divided into five provinces, called Divisions, and the capital of each division was the headquarters of a Resident. They therefore set sail for the little township of Limbang to call on the Resident of the Fifth Division. Arriving on the 29th November 1928, they were warmly welcomed by the Resident and his wife, two of the only three white people in the township. A few days later they were joined by Carey and Frank who sailed direct from Singapore.

The Resident generously made available to the party a Government bungalow at the outpost of Danau and gave them permission to stay there for three months. As they covered the thirty miles upriver to the outpost in a police launch they experienced for the first time the miles of muddy, meandering river with the endless dense green of palms on either bank, with which they would soon be so familiar. But their future journeys would not be in the comparative comfort and speed of a Government launch (the journey took only five hours, thanks to the favourable currents). They would be with the sweat and weariness of endless paddling of their own canoe, usually taking them two days.

Time was precious if they were to find somewhere to live within three months and by 19th December they were on their way, paddling further upriver. Within the first three days, as the mud and swamps gave way to various jungle trees and the water became clearer and faster flowing, they had met people from the four main tribes with whom they were to have contact over the next few years. First they met two canoes full of sturdy, rather travel-worn Kelabits. Their canoes, each hewn from a single tree trunk, had scarcely any free-board showing above the water, but such is the skill of these boatmen that there is usually very little danger that the boat will tip over. Just a taste of the future was given to the missionaries as they discovered that these Kelabits had taken three months on their journey from the far interior, due to high rivers and bad omens from the spirits.

The first night was spent at a Bisaya house where they slept for the first time on a split bamboo floor. The next day they moved out of Bisaya country into that occupied by Muruts (now called Lun Bawang). After thirteen miles of increasingly hard paddling, they reached a small Lun Bawang longhouse – a whole village living in one house. Here in the dingy light and with the lingering smell of rice beer, they attended a few sick people, stared at through the darkness by old and young alike. They put up their mosquito nets and settled down to try to sleep amidst the noises of dogs, crying babies, pigs under the house and, all too soon, cockerels crowing long before the dawn.

Next morning they were only able to progress two miles in over three hours because of the strong currents. Attempting to round a bend in the river, they were caught in a whirlpool and pushed back. It seemed not without significance that this happened just opposite a Lun Bawang burying ground which contained a thirty-foot totem pole, 'grotesquely carved,' – the first object of religious significance that they had seen.

Pressing on, they reached another Lun Bawang longhouse. This was nearly three hundred feet long, well built and 'displayed care and ingenuity'. They were well received, but their warmest welcome came from some Iban who called in to this house while they were there. These friendly people were somewhat taller than the Lun Bawang. With their strong bronzed bodies scantily clad with a loin cloth, the characteristic blue-grey tattooing on throat, shoulders, back, arms and thighs was clearly seen. They stood out as being 'a very fine type of people', and with such an escort the visiting party soon reached their first Iban longhouse. Tanah Merah was the largest house in the district.

'As we sat on their neatly-woven reed mats on the floor', wrote Hudson Southwell, 'we could see just above us two bunches of blackened human skulls, about twenty in all, while along the wall were hanging blowpipes and parangs [jungle knives].'

The people were very friendly. They talked freely and, ironically, the party came to the conclusion that 'the Iban stood out as being easiest of access for evangelism'. They did, however, observe that their attitude of friendliness seemed partly due to their desire for medical attention.

A year later Hudson wrote, 'These Iban from Tanah Merah are amongst our best friends now. . . we have frequently visited them and spent many nights in their house, generally for the purpose of treating their sick. They are hard workers and rise early . . . during the paddy season they are at work on their farms from early morning until late at night. . . At other seasons they make boats, build houses or hunt. . . . The old women . . . weave cloth, make mats and look after the younger children.' Then he added, 'They think of our worship only as a better method of invoking the aid of unseen powers. They have no thought of worshipping God as God, but only seek to obtain material benefits in response to their petitions . . . dreams and omens are of first importance in the ordering of their lives.'

On the return journey they looked for a suitable site for a house. Before leaving they had been instructed not to 'go native', a fact which caused them a certain amount of conflict. They certainly lived very roughly when travelling but while at Danau they felt they had to maintain a certain standard of living. Their need was to find somewhere where they could live under conditions that would enable

34

the tribespeople 'to understand that we have really come to them'.

Nevertheless, for their base they selected a site on a somewhat isolated hill on the opposite bank of the river to a small Lun Bawang community. By the new year permission had been granted for the base at Sungai Pranga and the Lun Bawang built them a small shelter, ten feet by twelve. There they lived for well over twelve months while they built themselves a more permanent house. Hudson related recently how they had read in *Daily Light* that 'the house that is to be builded for the Lord must be exceeding magnifical'. 'Of course,' Hudson added, 'we knew that it referred to the Church, but we took it to mean that we should build something solid and worthwhile.' Most of the work they had to do themselves. They levelled the ground, tongued and grooved the boards, with the result that it was mid-1930 before they were able to move in.

Writing during this time, Hudson voiced the frustration of each one, 'I would ask you to pray that we may soon be set free for more concentrated language study and missionary work. . . . All around are people who continually ask us to come and teach them. "How can we worship God", they ask, "if you do not teach us?" and we reply, "How can we teach you if we do not know your language?"'

They interspersed building with language learning and sorties in various directions. Carey Tolley concentrated his efforts on the Lubai, the next river to the north, where there were many Iban. He solved the problem of getting in among the people by building a little hut just alongside one of the longhouses, and from here he carried on an intensive programme of visitation. Not only did this enable him to learn Iban, but he was also able to learn much of their way of life and customs. Sometimes while staying in a longhouse, he was unexpectedly involved as a spectator to their pagan feasts.

These feasts were held to propitiate the spirits and seek the aid of Pulang Gana, their god of farming. With the noise and drinking which went on at such times, Carey could do little more than look on.

'Men, women and little boys of eight or ten years', he wrote, 'are seen hopelessly drunk. Young mothers leave their wee babies unattended all day long and these things make one sick at heart.'

Sometimes after waiting for two to three days for the uproar to cease, he would question them why they did these things. Their answer was always the same. It was their *adat* (custom) and 'all ordered by Pulang Gana'. The Iban *adat* was strong and binding.

Much time was given during that first year to the Iban, but during October 1929, Carey and Frank went out on a trip to the upper reaches of the Limbang and then walked overland for two days. They met 'a sturdy tribe of Kelabits who build their houses on the mountain tops' and also some Penan, 'the most primitive people of all'. The nomadic Penan 'build no houses but live in the jungle on jungle produce, they plant no paddy and do not know even how to cook rice. They live on wild fruit and animals, catching the latter with a blowpipe using deadly poisoned arrows.' The missionaries detected an open-heartedness among these shy jungle people.

Through their constant travelling, the team was gradually moving further inland, Hudson reaching the Medamit and Medalam rivers, both tributaries of the Limbang. He wrote in early 1930 of the 'Iban in the Lubai, Panderuan, Medamit and Medalam rivers . . . most of these have been visited at least once'. While Hudson and Carey concentrated on the Iban, Frank was becoming more and more burdened for the Kelabits, many of whom were intermittent visitors at Sungai Pranga. Frank had reached the stage of hoping to build a little hut for himself amongst the Kelabits of the Medihit (also a tributary of the

Limbang). It was six days upriver from Sungai Pranga and some six days walk from the main part of the tribe in the Highlands. Then there came a considerable setback.

Rajah Brooke had gone on leave to England and the Chief Secretary had charge of all affairs in his absence. During August 1930 he visited Limbang. While approving what was being done, he reiterated more firmly that 'the work of the Mission must be confined to the Limbang valley and not pressed too far inland, not at all into the mountains'.

Disappointed, the missionaries began to wonder whether this meant that God was turning their attention to the downriver Bisaya. There were 2,000 of them with other groups in the Tutong and Belait river area to the South. They were different from the Iban and had always been victims rather than aggressors. In appearance too they were different. They wore their long hair coiled around their heads while their filed teeth gave them a very distinctive appearance. Like the Iban they usually wore a loin-cloth but, being nearer the coast, some of them were beginning to wear an old pair of European shorts. The women wore just a long sarong tucked up under their armpits.

Hudson moved in to develop this work in July 1931, assisted by George Aitken, a new recruit. However, very little could be done beyond building a small hut on a hill site at Limpasong, before Hudson went on leave and to be married. George, carpenter turned pastor before leaving Australia, returned to Sungai Pranga to prepare the house for the first lady missionary to join the team.

Winsome arrived in 1932. She had been closely associated with all that had gone on in the early months of the formation of the BEM, particularly as many of the meetings between the founders had taken place in her aunt's front room. Delicate, beautiful and every inch a lady, Winsome seemed hardly suited to wading waist deep across rivers, climbing steep mountains and sleeping and eating on the floor of pagan longhouses. In fact, Hudson had been warned by a kindly friend that she was unlikely to last three months. But she knew God's call and has kept up with her indefatigable husband for nearly half a century of serving the Church in Borneo. Winsome quickly made the former bachelor quarters into a home with a few bits of pretty material and a feminine touch to the cooking. The Southwells then took over the base work at Sungai Pranga. They began a service on Sundays and morning prayers in Iban for those boys who were helping them. They read from the Iban New Testament which had already been translated, and one of them came to put his trust in the Lord. 'It's not what you've been saying, it's that Word,' was his comment.

Another new worker accompanied the Southwells on their return. Ro Bewsher's arrival meant that the Bisaya work could be reopened. But first he had to learn the trade language, Malay. This was no easy task, he recalls, on the isolated hill site where no one spoke Malay as his mother tongue; but this was not the greatest of the difficulties of those days. Ro arrived in the midst of the Depression.

'Funds were low in those days,' he explained. 'People at home had little money to spare for these young men hidden away in the jungles of Borneo.'

One month the official receipts for the Mission showed a transfer of £3 6s. 6d. for the month – all that could be sent to support six missionaries. They lived on rice and salt fish, with jungle vegetables and sometimes cheap tinned fish, and any birds or beasts which they could shoot. Thanks to permission to use gunpowder as currency, they were also able to barter for fresh meat and fish. A little bit of powered milk occasionally reminded them of the comforts of home, and even more occasionally they had the luxury of some chocolate.

Ro and George moved down to Limpasong at the end of

1932. 'We left – two of us – paddling ourselves in a small boat and carrying the bare essentials for life in the little leaf hut which Hudson had built before going on leave.' Of course they made frequent visits to the Bisaya houses around about but the prospect of response did not seem very great. Ro described in a letter home at the time the scene which greeted him one day as he approached a house:

'With bloodshot eyes and devilish gurgling voices, came those who could walk, their limp, sweaty hands outstretched in the formal meaningless greeting. . . . Oh, the sight! Swaying bodies squatting over earthenware jars and sucking with slavering lips through bamboo tubes at the potent rice spirit to which all this abandonment is due; and then lying in a drunken stupor upon the floor in grotesque postures . . . why all this? An intoxicated Bisaya explained, "This, Sir, is celebrating the death of my daughter."'

Shortly after this visit, George set off on a survey trip to the Tutong and Belait river areas, after receiving permission from the Brunei Government to work there. The main purpose of the journey was to ascertain the extent of the Bisayas but it was no easy journey. George wrote vividly in March 1933, describing the difficulties of finding a guide, probably partly due to the *paya* country through which they had to pass.

'The dictionary meaning of *paya* is marsh, bog, swamp; but most people add a large string of qualifying adjectives of their own and even then fail to describe it adequately. There is no solid ground in paya, just long, sharp grass growing in very liquefied mud. . . . As you step along, choosing the grass tussocks for each step, the coarse grass binds under your feet and stops you sinking out of sight. Even so, the average depth to which you sink is knee deep, before the grass binds sufficiently to hold your weight. Where the dictionary fails so lamentably to convey just what *paya* is, is that it cannot put in the leeches, the cuts and scratches that come from the sharp grass, and the tropical sun overhead, not only burning the body but causing nauseating odours to arise from the stagnant water that is all around.'

George went home in October 1934 for leave and regrettably illness prevented his return. Ro was thus left to carry on the Bisaya work alone. He needed to learn Bisaya, an unwritten language. He could not do this on the top of the hill at Limpasong, and thanks to a medical case he was brought into close contact with Itai and Lalang who lived half a mile downriver at Ranggu.

Ro decided to move to Ranggu for three months, not only to learn the language but to observe the Bisaya customs and culture. He was given a warm invitation to join the family and thus began a lasting friendship.

Rolling up his sleeping mat and collecting a few essential items (he deliberately left behind all reading material except his Bible) he paddled downstream and became a member of Itai's family for the next three valuable months.

'I was dark and of small stature,' he explained. 'This was an advantage. I tried to conform as much as possible to the life style of the people and to minimize my own foreignness. This I could not do completely as at the end of three months I still slept on the verandah as a visitor, but I was no longer an object of fear to the women and children and I was grateful.'

He had no dictionary, of course, no written language, no teacher and no linguistic training.

'I began like a child and learnt by absorption. I would sit for hours at a time with conversation going on around me, in total silence. Both in the house and out in the fields working with the family, I gradually began to recognize sounds and words and fairly rapidly I began to get a working knowledge of the language.'

It had all been very worthwhile for not long after Ro

returned to Limpasong, Itai and Lalang came to the house. 'We want to become Christians,' they announced, and together with their two older boys they gave their hearts to the Lord. The family has remained the nucleus of the Bisaya church to this day.

* * * * *

Such joys were few and far between in those early days. Frank, writing after a last visit to the Kelabits before going on leave in 1932, spoke of his disappointment that he could not see some harvest before leaving. Carey, about the same time, wrote of the Iban remaining friendly but unwilling to commit themselves to Christianity. At Tanah Merah he had spoken with some feeling of his sadness that not one of them had come to trust in God.

'Well, Sir,' one of them had replied, 'do not take it so much to heart. We will believe one day.'

Reporting this, Carey added, no doubt speaking for all the missionaries,

'It takes faith to continue in a work such as this, but we can go on as we look off to Jesus.'

There is one sentence in this letter, the significance of which could not have been seen at the time. Carey goes on to remark that 'they want to believe a household at a time, but cannot yet see that this is not God's way, the "Narrow Way"'.

Four years' hard grind and very little to show. But then in 1933 God granted a tremendous encouragement to the missionaries and the sort of revolution to their thinking that J. O. Fraser[1] had experienced amongst the Lisu tribespeople who live in the hills of S.W. China and Northern Burma. God had led him to pray for whole families, not just for individuals, and then had drawn thousands of Lisu to turn from paganism to trust in Christ.

In 1933 God began a similar movement amongst the

[1] *Behind the Ranges*, J. O. Fraser, OMF.

Lun Bawang; not the Lun Bawang of the Limbang but those who lived along the Trusan river which flows from the mountains near the Indonesian border into Brunei Bay to the north-east of the Limbang. The Lun Bawang in the Limbang had given a polite hearing to the missionaries, but those in the Trusan were desperately hungry to hear of this new way to God.

CHAPTER 4

FIRST LIGHT

THE Lun Bawang were drunk one hundred days out of every 365, according to the *Sarawak Gazette*. They were dying out. In the past they had been both prosperous and numerous, but when headhunting was abolished by law under the rule of the White Rajah these former warriors had time on their hands. The Lun Bawang men no longer had to guard the farms while the women worked. Always hospitable, they entertained even more lavishly and at every marriage, death festival and other celebration they drank jar after jar of rice beer. The celebrations would last for days and even small children would take part. In fact only the dogs were sober.

Inevitably their farms were neglected and their houses became filthy. According to Mr Banks, curator of the Sarawak Museum, 'the upriver Murut was more often drunk than not, his house indescribably filthy, covered in soot and cobwebs, the floor showing traces of recent debauches, dogs everywhere, pigs under the house in a general "lavatory after a gale of wind effect"'. Visiting medical officers were appalled at their disease-ridden bodies and they had no resistance to epidemics which were frequent and severe. Since the beginning of the century, the population had been rapidly declining.

The BEM missionaries had had occasional contact with the Lun Bawang and in May 1933 Carey Tolley felt very burdened to visit them. However, after consultation with a Government officer he decided to visit the upriver Kelabits. But he found himself faced again with the challenge of the Lun Bawang when he met a man from Ba Kelalan, which is near the border with Dutch (now

Indonesian) Borneo. This man had a strange story to tell. He and some friends had met a white man while they were visiting friends in Indonesia and he had told them 'a wonderful story about God who had a Son named Jesus who would be returning to this earth again to take them up to heaven'. Of course this white man, W. E. Prestwood, an American of the Christian and Missionary Alliance, had told them many other things but it was not surprising that the Lun Bawang, living in his filth and degradation, despised by all other tribes in Borneo, had gripped hold of the idea of escape to heaven. Some had even decided to give up farming altogether and wait for Jesus to come. The news had spread far and wide and with it some very peculiarly garbled versions of the truth. Some believed that God would put ropes under their longhouses and take them all up to heaven, but what God was going to do with their filthy houses in heaven, no one really knew!

Carey knew he must go without delay and on 24th June he set off to cross the watershed between the upper reaches of the Limbang, where the Kelabits lived, to Lun Bawang country in the upper reaches of the river Trusan. For three days they did not meet with any habitation and Carey's heart and mind were 'stirred with thoughts of God's power and majesty' as he looked out on 'range upon range of magnificent mountains'. He was about to see the beginnings of God's power at work among the Lun Bawang.

Having crossed the watershed, they descended into the Trusan valley and then followed the Kelalan, a tributary of the Trusan, up to the Indonesian border. People gathered from near and far to hear what the missionary had to say.

'During our whole time in Borneo', Carey wrote when he returned, 'I have never seen anything to approach it . . . they kept coming to hear more . . . one could hear a pin drop' (most unusual in a Lun Bawang or any other longhouse!) 'so intent were they on not missing anything'.

Some who had been over to Indonesian Borneo expressed amazement that what they were hearing was exactly what they had heard from the white man over there, and Carey had difficulty in convincing them that he had not had a letter from Prestwood. He was eventually able to explain to them that both he and Prestwood had the same Book – God's revelation to man.

When the people expressed a desire to follow Jesus all together, not just in ones and twos, Carey was quite concerned and he explained that God did not want lip service but heart obedience. They understood, and still insisted they wanted to follow Jesus. It was the same in every village. The people left their farms, their work, whatever they were doing, to come and listen and there was scarcely any time to eat or sleep.

Gradually too Carey discovered the source of some of the strange rumours. Prestwood had had to speak by interpretation, and some who had interpreted for him had distorted the message. After he had left, others had deliberately caused confusion and one man in particular had tried to draw them back to the old ways. However, not long after this he had died and this had had a profound effect on the people. Carey returned by the way he had come in order to revisit every house and straighten out the confusion. It was a timely trip, he felt, as he made for home.

It was not yet over, however. He met three Lun Bawang by the wayside. They were actually waiting for him! They took him back to the nearby longhouse where a Lun Bawang chief was waiting with ten others. They showed him a long stick with 72 marks on it, made by those who had come from various houses along the Trusan valley to see him. Most had had to go back to their farms, but they had left their friends to bring Carey over to teach them. Needless to say, Carey did not hesitate.

The hunger was even greater than in the Ba Kelalan area.

'It brought tears to one's eyes to hear young and old, men and women, boys and girls alike, confessing their desire to trust and follow Jesus', he wrote. 'The sweet musical tones of their language sounded all the sweeter when . . . used to name the sweetest Name in Heaven and upon earth. Their words still ring in my ears, *Kai sikal harap ka Tuhan Isa* (We desire to believe in the Lord Jesus).'

While Carey was away visiting these Lun Bawang of the Upper Trusan, the Southwells at Sungai Pranga had unexpected visitors. In a letter dated 20th July, Hudson wrote home,

'One day last week, on returning to the house, I found three men, strangers, waiting for me. . . . They came from the Trusan and the journey had taken them a week. After the usual formalities, I told them why we were here – to tell people about God. "That's why we have come to see you," said one man, Raut, who seemed to be the leader.'

Raut was in fact a headman, and he and his people from the lower Trusan had been hearing similar rumours to those which were stirring the Lun Bawang upriver. 'Some I believe and some I don't,' Raut continued, 'and I want to find out the truth.'

Hudson went on to explain the Gospel to them and the three men listened intently, often breaking in with gasps of wonder. They seemed astonished that the missionaries had been there so long and yet everyone had not believed and followed God.

'How can they put more value on this life in comparison with what God offers?' Raut asked, and Hudson commented in his letter, 'It seemed that his mind had been opened and God had taught him; many times I was surprised at his spiritual understanding and grasp of things . . . seekers such as this may be common in other lands but they are most unusual here.'

They asked how they could pray to this God and, as has

46

happened so often up and down the hills and valleys of Borneo as tribespeople have passed on the good news, Hudson did not give them a long discourse. He closed his eyes and began to talk to God. They listened and learned and, after receiving a promise of a visit as soon as possible, returned to tell their friends.

Hudson set out on 14th August, travelling overland, crossing the Lubai and Panderuan rivers, scene of Carey's work amongst the Iban. He found the first signs of real hunger in a Lun Bawang village on the next river, the Batu Apui, and Hudson contrasted their concern with the polite interest of the Limbang Lun Bawang. From there they pressed on to the Trusan 'through the wildest part of the whole journey – beautiful mountains and valleys, but so dense that one felt in a peculiar way the loneliness and the unknown depths of the primitive Bornean forest'.

As they emerged into the good open country before descending to the Trusan valley, the guide explained to Hudson that thirty years before there had been hundreds of Lun Bawang there, but a fearful scourge of smallpox had wiped them out. They reached the Trusan and that night over 60 crowded onto the verandah of the house to hear the message. Next day they went on to Raut's house some five hours away, poling up rapids. Here Hudson experienced a foretaste of things to come as Raut interpreted for him. 'I understood enough to know that what he said was a free translation of what I had said, but it took on new life in his speech, carrying the conviction of his own heart.' Lun Bawang were going to preach to Lun Bawang in the absence of the missionaries.

It was the same story at every longhouse as Hudson returned downriver and made his way back to Limbang by sea. He estimated that, with 56 longhouses in the downriver section and 35 in the upriver section visited by Carey, there were at least 2,000 people wanting to become

Christians, in addition to some 300 in the Ba Kelalan area. It was essential that they should be taught immediately and Carey made a further visit.

This time he followed Hudson's route across to the Trusan and then headed upriver to Ba Kelalan and back. There were very many sick people whom he was able to help as he travelled upriver, but it was pneumonic flu from which they were suffering, and these sickly Lun Bawang had very little resistance to it. As he returned he was greatly distressed to find that many had died while he had been travelling, but in spite of this the others still wanted to become Christians. Some had died calling on the name of Jesus.

Eventually by February 1934 permission had been given to make occasional visits to the Trusan, but the Government made it quite clear that they wanted to see a school established in the Limbang before allowing extension of a permanent nature. But then there was a setback. A change of Government officers led to withdrawal of permission even to visit the Trusan, ironically the very month that the opening of the school was announced to the Iban and Lun Bawang of the Limbang.

'We couldn't possibly let you go among them. They are dangerous', the Resident in Limbang had explained to them. Later in the year a further request was made, this time to the Resident in Miri, but he too refused. The following year, Rajah Vyner Brooke himself was visiting Limbang and the missionaries went to see him. But probably the Rajah had recently received a report from one of his District Officers saying that the Lun Bawang 'have decreased disastrously since the last time due to epidemics, and appear to be doomed'.

The Rajah's reply was to let them die out, that younger and better people should be worked with, that they were 'old boots' and beyond hope.

Recollecting this years later, Hudson told how the three of them had gone home, paddling hard well into the night to relieve their pent-up feelings. They had seen a pig and shot it, and as they sat on the river bank round their fire eating roast pig, he had got out his *Daily Light*.

'Sit still, my daughter,' he had read, and they concluded that God who had given them this feast of pig at a time of great shortage, could open the door to the Lun Bawang.

* * * * * *

While the door remained fast closed to the Lun Bawang, the missionaries sought other doors for outreach, with only glimpses of light to encourage them. There were four main lines of advance – Iban, Bisaya, Kelabit and a quite separate development into Sabah which will be discussed in chapter seven.

Carey returned to the Lubai in 1935 with his new wife Florence and continued there for three years. There was not much fruit, but one young man who became a Christian then was recently reported as 'still preaching Christ to the Iban in the Lubai' nearly forty years later. The Southwells moved into the heart of Iban country, a day's journey upriver from Sungai Pranga where they spent a couple of years, ministering to the medical needs of the 33-family longhouse Nanga Meruyu and conducting a school for the young people. Looking back over that time the BEM Annual Report for 1939 concludes that 'the stay of the Southwells amongst the people has only served to emphasize the hardness of the Iban heart'. However, during that time the Southwells had again spent many hours reading to the people from the Iban New Testament, and the words did not go unheeded. Thirty years later the Southwells revisited Nanga Meruyu, and they found 'men and women welcoming us, not only socially and, as it were, for the sake of old times but because they had attended our

49

school when they were children. "We still remember the words," they said, meaning of course the Bible.'

Among the Bisaya, following the decision of Itai and Lalang, there were some real signs of response. Ro Bewsher had continued to master the Bisaya language, had translated Mark's Gospel and made a start on John. He had prepared reading primers and other small leaflets, and the small school at Limpasong had seen the training of what would be some of the future leaders of the Church in Borneo. But perhaps the most significant event was that Itai and Lalang, having been almost silent believers for nearly three years, began to witness to their fellow Bisayas. Helped of course by Ro, they saw over thirty make a profession of faith during 1938. This number included two headmen and some witch doctors. By 1939, the Ranggu church had appointed four officers and assumed full responsibility for all its affairs.

The door which was closed to the Lun Bawang, was also closed to the Kelabits. The Government reiterated yet again the attitude towards advance in that direction which it had expressed earlier. 'The Government considers the Kelabits to be somewhat treacherous and has not viewed with favour the idea of a white man living amongst them.'[1] This was in spite of the fact that the Kelabits of the Medihit had given a piece of land in 1932, so that Frank could come and build a house near to their longhouse. The Report goes on to say, 'Pray that in the Lord's time permission for this will be given.'

That time came earlier for the Kelabits than for the Lun Bawang. After Frank's return from leave in June 1934 and by the time his bride-to-be was crossing the seas from Melbourne, he had gone to build his little hut.

[1] BEM Annual Report 1939.

50

CHAPTER 5

OUT ON A LIMB

'THE house has been left since January, so maybe Frank won't be able to find it,' Enid Davidson wrote in August 1935. She was thinking of the lush jungle growth which takes over rapidly and relentlessly in Borneo. Enid had arrived in February and, after a few months of orientation and language learning, she was ready to go with Frank to the Medihit. But there had been so much talking, negotiating and changing of plans by the local Iban and Lun Bawang men who were to take them, that finally they could get only enough crew for Frank to set off without his wife.

Perhaps it was just as well. On arrival he found that 'the jungle has repossessed the clearing and it was only possible to reach the little building with difficulty and after receiving many cuts from the sharp grass'. He had to prise open the bark door to get into the house.

Once in, he found other occupants. Two large and dangerous snakes had taken up residence in the home to which he had intended to bring his young bride! It was only after some tense moments that they were able to dispose of the intruders. Frank then spent a few days getting the house habitable again and renewing old friendships with the Kelabits. In spite of the difficulties he was eager to get back to collect his wife and to start on this new venture.

Frank loved pioneering and, according to a colleague, he was 'perhaps happiest in his ministry in the Medihit amongst his beloved Kelabits'. He had already begun to learn their unwritten language and had closely identified with their tribal life-style. As they shot down the rapids, he

51

was no passenger. His powerful voice could be heard above the roar of the water, whooping, shouting and jesting in typical Kelabit style along with all the rest. He loved poling up the rapids too, and was quite at home hunting wild pig, either with a party or alone. The Kelabits felt he belonged to them.

On several occasions, he arrived unexpectedly at some remote village. There was sudden consternation as the people thought the visitors were a Government party on patrol, and they were not ready for them. Then, as Frank himself appeared, there was instant relief and the shout 'Tuan tau luk idi' (It's our tuan). He was also their teacher and counsellor. Problems and disputes were patiently dealt with well into the night, after travelling and preaching were done.

At last in September 1935 Frank was on his way to the Medihit again, this time taking his wife with him. Enid, not long out of University life in Melbourne and married just seven months, was the first white woman to visit the Medihit. It took six days of poling, paddling and dragging of boats up rapids to reach this group of Kelabits. Enid wrote home to tell of her experiences on this first journey.

'I did not have a very good sleep', she wrote, describing their first night-stop in a Lun Bawang longhouse. 'There was too much noise – cats fighting, babies crying, pigs grunting and roosters crowing. One of the women was up cooking about 4 a.m. [a situation with which she would soon become very familiar] and the light of the fire kept me awake.'

The next day was all rapids and by the evening they had left all signs of habitation behind. After a rather wet night in a small leaf shelter quickly erected in the jungle on the bank of the river, they entered the gorge, passing a huge limestone rock, some hundred feet high. Here the river becomes much narrower and swifter and the rapids are so steep that the boats have to be dragged.

But the journey provided much opportunity to admire the skills of these river-dwelling people. As they reach the top of the rapids, they jump back into the boat with almost precision timing, but there is no fear of unduly wobbling the unstable craft. Paddling furiously, or poling, they move away from the rushing water and then comes the compensation of gliding along in calm water. Born and bred by the rivers, these men can stand with perfect balance in a wobbly dug-out canoe. As they pole it is only the tension in their strong, muscular shoulders that gives any indication that it is not with effortless ease they plough through the fast-flowing waters.

After the Davidsons, on this occasion, had spent another two nights sleeping on stones at the river's edge, they finally reached the Medihit about lunchtime on the sixth day. But here the going was even harder, each rapid taking about fifteen minutes. Before the last long bend of the river Frank decided his wife needed a break, so they took a short cut overland. They could see the house through the six-foot-long grass and reached it half an hour ahead of the boats which had continued to battle their way through the rapids.

'I think we will be very comfortable in our little house,' the bride wrote as she contemplated their first home. It was built up on stilts as are all Kelabit houses. This was originally done for defence purposes, but it was very convenient to maintain the habit when their houses were built lower down the mountains; rivers can flood very rapidly in the heavy rainfall of Borneo. It was made of bark and consisted of one room with a small separated kitchen where Enid would learn to cook on an open wood fire. The stairs were made of two logs with other logs tied across with rattan cane to form steps. (Frank had decided to dispense with the more normal notched log which could be lifted up on to the verandah at night to prevent intruders.) There being no nails in the interior, the whole house was tied together with split rattan cane, the posts being just the trunks of trees.

They had been fortunate to make the journey without delays. On subsequent journeys they were not so fortunate, but they continually experienced God's protection and provision. When on one occasion they were delayed for several days by a high river they just 'happened' to have brought some extra rice with them, and one of the men had been able to shoot a deer. On that occasion the shelter that the men had made for themselves near the edge of the river had been washed away by the rising water, but fortunately the men themselves had moved in time.

Going downstream was often more dangerous than going up and as all these early missionaries were constantly on the move, each one had stories to tell of the Lord's amazing protection. Enid speaks for them all as she describes one journey in a high river. They had their first narrow escape when they were caught between two whirlpools and the water from both of them came pouring into the canoe.

Then later that same day they came to a place where there were huge rocks right across the river. These were only visible in low water. 'We missed them all but the last one which was just covered by the rushing water,' Enid wrote. 'We were shooting down and before the men could bring the boat clear, we had raced on to this huge rock. The front of the boat was up in the air out of the water.'

Frank tried to jump out but had to get back in quickly as the water was too deep and swift to get any sort of footing. The boat swayed on the rock. For a few seconds that seemed like minutes, or even hours, no one quite knew what to do. They were expecting any second to be turned out into the swirling waters. Eventually the men in front managed to work the boat off the rock and they were on their way again, thanking God for their deliverance.

'We looked back at the big rock and realized that it was a miracle the boat had not split in two,' was Enid's comment.

There were of course more than just physical problems connected with living in such an isolated spot. Omens controlled most aspects of life for the Kelabits. They had to wait for a favourable omen before they could choose a site for a house, and might well have to abandon the project later even though the house was half built. A beautiful boat might be left to be eaten by white ants, even if it was nearing completion, should a bird be heard or a snake seen. Omens might cause delays in farming which could be disastrous. The rice would have to be left to rot on the ground – famine would result, but 'it is better to starve than to offend the spirits'. A child might be given away or even left to die if a deer was heard to bark during its birth, and a person would certainly die out of sheer terror as a result of a bad omen or disobedience to any message from the spirits.

Journeys could be delayed for days or even months. It is most informative to see the great variety of things which on one occasion caused a delay from 15th September to 12th December. Enid's diary reads:

'*15th September 1935*. Balang Imat and others going to coast to pay headtax. Before setting out they watch the eagles. If the eagle circles round and round, it is a good omen, but if it drops in its flight they will not travel. If the eagle approaches you on the left, it is a bad omen whereas if it approaches you on the right, it is a good omen.

23rd October. Balang Imat now says he is going next month.

15th November. Balang had set out, had a bad omen so returned home. After 3 days he can set out again. Government are talking of sending one of the Penghulus up to see why the Kelabits haven't paid their taxes.

24th November. Balang expecting to leave tomorrow – 4 boatloads of Kelabits.

25th November. Balang had a bad omen. They started on their way but two snakes crossed their path so they had to turn back.

26th November. Today the river is up. The Kelabits will not start on a journey if it is raining early in the morning.

30th November. Balang hasn't gone yet. They have been waiting a week. Another bad omen – one old man Pun Tai saw a bird or heard one, and so all had to stay. . . . Balang wanted to go, but would he dare run the risk of an accident, by disobeying the warnings of the bird? . . . When the rest of the company wanted to go Pun Tai threatened them with certain death.

Balang Imat asked Frank for medicine for their bad omens . . . Frank told him how to trust in God . . .

1st December. Kelabits . . . reached the mouth of the Medihit river, but a girl had died that night at the house at the mouth of the river so they had to turn back.

12th December. 7 boatloads of Kelabits left for the coast.'

The Davidsons' mail was totally dependent on the travelling of the Kelabits and this made living in these lonely and isolated areas none too easy for those who had been used to the comforts of life and easy communications of Australia. Looking back over the years, Enid recollected how they would run down to the river when they heard the shouting of a boatload of Kelabits nearing their landing stage.

'Would they have any mail for us? Had they called at Sungai Pranga or had they passed by?' And after many, many years, Enid added, 'I shall never forget the excitement, the anticipation of mail arriving.' This was hardly surprising when we realize that it was often three to four months since the previous mail. One year, they had a mail in January and then the next mail arrived in June. On

Pagan longhouse

that occasion the Kelabits who had been down at the coast had been delayed for six weeks by flood water.

The Davidsons worked and travelled from their tiny home in the Medihit until their leave in August 1938. They learnt the language, taught a few to read and translated some simple Bible stories. They constantly visited the longhouses nearby and did a great deal of medical work, including treating occasional nomadic Penans whom they met from time to time. Obviously every opportunity was taken to tell them of the One who could free them from the fear of spirits. But at the end of it all the annual report for 1938–1939 tells of the lack of any definite response. 'A church, a school and many Kelabit Christians are what is requested of the Lord. . . . It is possible to find Kelabits seeking the Saviour when the Davidsons return next year.'

That is exactly what happened. Then the Davidsons were faced with the most difficult dilemma of the whole of their time in Borneo. It was because God had answered prayer more abundantly than any had even dared to hope.

PART 2

DAYBREAK

1938–1950

Harvesting rice

CHAPTER 6

LUN BAWANG MIRACLE

BEHIND the closed door to the Lun Bawang God had been working, while friends in Australia and of course the missionaries had continued to pray. Towards the end of 1937 reports began to reach the missionaries that there had been a change in the Lun Bawang, and this prompted a renewed urgency in their praying.

13th November 1937 was set aside by the whole Borneo Fellowship as a Day of Prayer. This was the turning point. One week later 'immediate permission to enter the Trusan for missionwork' had been granted by the Rajah himself. By January 1938 Carey Tolley was on his way to the Trusan to find a suitable site for a house from which to visit the Lun Bawang. All went well and unusually quickly with the building, thanks to a friendly Chinese who was at least a nominal Christian, but the situation with the Lun Bawang was not at first so bright.

'Sickness off and on through the past four years has greatly reduced their numbers,' Carey wrote. 'Some houses have lost more than fifty per cent. Only a few hundreds are left, those fast drinking themselves into the grave.'

Upriver, however, the situation was brighter, although sickness had taken its toll there too. When these upriver Lun Bawang had found that the missionaries were not able to return to them they had sent over to Indonesia for someone to come and teach them. Panai Ruab, a Lun Bawang from Sabah who had already gone to Indonesia, had become a Christian while there and he and others had responded to the call. The Lun Bawang had listened to the message and had begun radically to change their whole pattern of living.

There was obviously need for much teaching. Carey reported that while he was building his house he had visitors on two occasions telling him that the upriver Lun Bawang were 'trying to follow what I had taught them but have forgotten a lot'.

Carey was eager to visit them, but having built a suitable little house he was forced by ill-health to go on leave on 23rd March 1938. Sadly, while at home, the Tolleys felt they had to resign from the Mission 'for health and family reasons'. This was a great tragedy at such a critical time, especially as a few months after they had left further news came that 'three houses in the headwaters of the Trusan are reported to be living apart from heathen practices'. It was urgent to visit them but Frank, who spoke Kelabit, a closely related language, had also just gone on leave.

Stafford Young, the donor of that original £50 during the embryo stage of the Mission, had visited the missionaries in 1935. Seeing the urgent need for more personnel, he had stayed on to help. He did not speak Lun Bawang but he seemed to be the only one available to go. He set off in December 1938, taking with him Lawai, a young Lun Bawang who had become a Christian through the Southwells' ministry at Sungai Pranga. Stafford described him as 'not very bright as a Christian, but he was willing to go and interpret'. Also in the party were four pagan Lun Bawang men to act as carriers. The Government District Officer reluctantly agreed to the trip and sent them off with many forebodings.

Stafford soon discovered that the reports which had been coming from the Upper Trusan had told only half the story. He wrote of his growing excitement as he progressed upriver. Instead of their little party of six, there were often twenty or thirty Lun Bawang following them from village to village. They would carry the men's loads for them for the sheer love of it, 'an unheard of thing' at that stage in the Mission's experience.

When they reached a village, crowds flocked round them to hear what they had to say and to listen to the explanations of the Gospel pictures. Then there would be a barrage of questions touching every phase of life.

'What does God say on this?'

'What shall we do in that case? What does God say?'

'It was awe-inspiring,' Stafford continued, 'to realize the whole tribal mind was open to God's wishes and instructions. In other districts the heathen mind is closed to anything new, fast barred with the iron of age-old custom and superstition.'

The visitors were amazed to hear the prayers of these people last thing at night, and they were awakened by the same chorus of prayer before the break of dawn. Stafford observed:

'At home prayer is so often laboured. Young Christians have to be urged to pray in front of others. Not so in the isolated jungles of Borneo. With no direct teacher other than the Holy Spirit, these people pour out spontaneous, full-hearted prayer.'

Could it all be true or was it perhaps just put on for the sake of the visitors? Stafford knew the touchstone to the Lun Bawang way of life and he decided to test them out.

'Where is your *borak* [rice beer] now?' he asked.

'Oh, we've given that up long ago.'

'What about betel nut chewing and tobacco?'

'That too,' was the answer.

During the whole month's trip he did not see any signs of these things.

'It was hard to believe. When a whole tribe in heathendom can give up of themselves the usual narcotic aids to living, including third-degree drinking, the movement actuating them must be more than superficial. I soon came to the conclusion, the one that remains with us all on the Field – it was God!'

God was showing to the BEM that although He

63

delighted to use them as the scaffolding to this building He, and He alone, was the Builder.

Stafford continued: 'There was spiritual power. I had with me one indifferent Christian and four heathen. What of them? The first, Lawai, got on fire for God and on return asked for baptism; two of the others trusted Christ; the pace (spiritually) was too hot for the other two; they cleared out without their wages! Those friendly Lun Bawang soon filled the gap; in fact we came home nine strong instead of our outward five – filled with praises to God.'

A few months later Hudson Southwell was able to make the second trip and he too was amazed at the change.

'In 1933 they were drunken but eager for the Gospel, now they were healthy and clean. When we got to Long Semadoh we found a beautifully clean, new longhouse, no pigs. You could walk underneath.'

It so happened that they met with a Government party at Long Semadoh, the new District Officer, together with Mr Banks, Curator of the Sarawak Museum. They had also gone to investigate whether the reports of changes really were true.

'What on earth have you done to these people, Southwell?' was Banks' greeting. He suggested that they write an article on the subject for the *Sarawak Gazette*.

'Not I,' replied Hudson. 'You wrote about them when they were drunk. You write now you see them changed.' And he did, light-heartedly commenting that 'the place was so swept up that there was no place to put the used banana skins. . . . The Trusan Murut (Lun Bawang) house, from being the foulest in Sarawak . . . is now quite the cleanest and best kept.'[1]

God had turned the tribe to Himself. Debilitating drinking feasts had been replaced by daily prayer meetings and hymn singing. The crippling fear of spirits was

[1] *Sarawak Gazette*, 1st July 1939.

changed to a holy fear of God. The adultery and promiscuity which had helped to spread disease, had been done away with. New values of hygiene and cleanliness had become important.

The Government, having refused permission for five years to establish work amongst the Lun Bawang, now began to press hard for advantage to be taken of the great change in the situation.

*   *   *   *   *

The Davidsons returned from leave in August 1939, believing that the time had come when they would see a harvest among the Kelabits. The missionary team, meeting in conference that year, saw the urgent need for an experienced missionary to go to teach the thousands of 'babes in Christ' among the Lun Bawang, and they felt that Frank and Enid should be the ones to go. There was no one else available.

The Davidsons were torn. Frank made a visit through Lun Bawang country and then on to the Medihit to see the situation for himself. The needs of the Lun Bawang were critical and he longed to help. But then what they had been longing for among the Kelabits happened. With the return of their missionary, one whole longhouse and several smaller groups turned to Christianity. They too needed to be taught. The Davidsons were 'bewildered and distressed' as they battled with the longing to go and teach the Kelabits whom they knew and loved so well. Yet the need was far greater for the Lun Bawang.

It was God who had brought this group of Kelabits to Himself. But it was also God who had worked such an incredible miracle among the Lun Bawang. God was the builder and He must know how best to use the scaffolding in the building of His church. Frank turned to the Lord, as he always did, to find out what His will was.

'I delight to do thy will, O my God' is a verse which Enid

said recently she will always associate with Frank. It had been the key to his ministry for many years and Enid recalls her 'lasting picture of Frank sitting at his desk at 5 o'clock each morning, reading by the light of his hunting lamp, deep in prayer as he sought God's will for the day and His enabling power'. God gave the Davidsons the assurance that it was His will that they should move to the Lun Bawang, but that they should spend three to four months teaching the Kelabits first.

There was so much to do during those few precious months. There were endless calls for teaching even from as far away as the Kelabit Highlands. While the Southwells were visiting the Davidsons in early 1940, Frank and Hudson were able to travel into the Highlands where they found a great interest for teaching. There was, however, no real desire to respond, except in one man Pun Abi. He was willing to commit himself and stood up on their last night of preaching.

'I don't mind what anyone else does, I'm going to trust in Jesus,' he said and he stood firm all through the war years until the missionaries were able to return.

Back in the Medihit, Frank continued to translate portions of Scripture and to teach the young men in his little school to read them. Sunday services were held and the Davidsons found it a great joy to hear these Kelabits singing hymns translated into their own language, and to see the Lord working in their hearts. Among them was also a young Lun Bawang lad, Racha Umong, who would one day become the Chairman of the whole Evangelical Church in Borneo and a member of the Federal Parliament of Malaysia. How disappointing it was to have to close down such a work, but with so few missionaries there seemed to be no alternative. They left, promising that they would continue to visit the Kelabits from time to time.

The Davidsons arrived in the township of Trusan on the lower Trusan river, in April 1940. Later that year they visited Lawas, another downriver trading centre for the Lun Bawang about half a day's journey away. It was an administrative centre, and the Rajah himself was making a visit. The Rajah could hardly believe what he saw when he arrived.

'I am amazed at the change in the Murut [Lun Bawang],' he said. 'I believe you have done more good in a few years than Government has done in forty.' He went on to say how impressed he was with 'that little lady' (meaning Enid Davidson) surrounded by forty or fifty Lun Bawang men, women and children. 'I've never seen anything like it before,' he said. 'Obviously they have the confidence of the people and a great influence over them. Yet the thing that surprised me is that your Mission does all this by methods of faith and by spiritual means.'[1]

The Davidsons had come at God's command, to meet a need, but the task that faced them was overwhelming.

'The need here is frightening,' Enid wrote. 'Thousands of Christians to be guided and taught.' But they were happy to be there. As Enid looked back over the dilemma in which they had been she commented recently,

'Once we had moved to the Trusan we felt it was God's place for us and we learned to love the Lun Bawang and longed for them to grow in knowledge and grace.' But the task for just two people was nevertheless daunting.

In God's amazing providence, it was the Japanese invasion of Borneo in December 1941 which provided extra help for this enormous task. At first, though, it looked even more desperate. Due to the tense situation in the months prior to the invasion, Enid had been ordered home by the Government as she was expecting their second child. Frank was joined by a new missionary, Brian Morcombe, who had arrived just a month before Japan entered the war, but of course he did not speak the language. Frank pressed on and God gave him nine

[1] BEM Twelfth Annual Report.

valuable months for teaching and establishing the churches.

When the Japanese landed in Miri, Frank was asked to lead a party of Europeans into the interior to 'hide'. Frank did not like the idea of retreating, but fortunately he was prevailed upon to withdraw 'to continue his missionary work' at Berayong halfway between the coast and the Indonesian border. Had they stayed in the coastal region, they would have been interned.

Representatives of each of the interior churches came to the school which Frank set up and there they were not only taught but, as Frank translated the Gospel of Luke, each one wrote out his own copy. When the missionaries had to surrender in October 1942 they knew that every church had a literate member who could read his handwritten copy of Luke's Gospel. Frank had also translated several other books of the New Testament.

The additional help in the teaching came from the Southwells, who were on the border of Indonesian Borneo and could not return to their base. They conducted similar schooling, baptizing many believers and establishing deacons in the churches. Even more help came in May when they were joined by a young missionary, John Willfinger, a gifted linguist of the Christian and Missionary Alliance who were working in Indonesia. He and the Southwells produced Mark's Gospel and they left a typed copy behind with the Lun Bawang. Winsome took another copy into internment with her and was able to keep it hidden from the Japanese. Once she had to hide it under the washing out on the line when there was an inspection. It was never found and so could be printed after the war was over.

The Lun Bawang pleaded with both parties not to surrender, but when it became obvious that they were endangering the lives of their Lun Bawang friends, the decision was made. John Willfinger crossed the border and surrendered to the Japanese at the coast. He was kept in confinement for about six weeks and then shot.

The Southwells, Frank and Brian had a sad but triumphal journey down to the coast on the Sarawak side. They held services at the different villages, questioned and baptized hundreds of believers, and appointed leaders and deacons in the various churches.

The Lun Bawang were to be left once again, but this time they had had some concentrated teaching, and they had small portions of the Bible. They would prove yet again that they could survive, even though all human props were gone, because God was with them.

CHAPTER 7

ADVANCE AND . . . BARBED WIRE

Gᴏᴅ called a reluctant replacement for the Davidsons. Madge Hill had been ill for some time and felt quite happy that God would not call her overseas, although she was interested in praying for Borneo. Then she read the report in the *BEM Newsletter* that the Davidsons were having to move from the Kelabits.

'Who's going to replace them?' was the thought that flashed through her mind, and to her astonishment she felt an overwhelming conviction that God was calling her.

On looking back after a period of frequent visits to the Kelabits, teaching in the Bible School and then translating the Lun Bawang Bible, Madge recalled,

'I didn't go out nobly. I had rebelled against my call for five years.'

But maybe God overruled for good through her reluctance. Being so frail at the time, she could well not have survived internment. Even after the war, when Alan Belcher had asked her to marry him, one friend expressed real doubt as to whether she would make the grade, just as others had wondered about Winsome Southwell. But when she finally left for Borneo, she passed her medical and she and Alan have spent many long periods in arduous travel and rough living.

It's hard to believe that such a rugged, hard-working man as Alan Belcher might also have been turned down on health grounds. He had had TB in his youth. But surprisingly, on examination, he was found to be completely clear. But there were other obstacles.

As has happened with others in the BEM team, and indeed so often happens when a man or woman starts to move towards service for God, he was offered most attractive promotion. He was asked to become the New Zealand manager of his firm. Although not knowing the attitude of his present manager, Alan nevertheless agreed to accept the job only if he was turned down by the BEM. To Alan's surprise, the manager agreed. He was a devout Jew.

'A good name is more important than wealth,' he commented.

'I think so too,' the younger man agreed.

'I'm not asking you what you think. I am telling you the truth,' the manager replied.

C. H. Nash had also tried to stop Alan from applying to the BEM. By this time the Mission had become fully Field directed, and he felt that the move had been premature. Alan, however, persisted in his efforts to go to Borneo, in spite of his high regard for the opinion of so revered a Christian leader. After twelve months of trying other avenues, Alan returned to Mr Nash who then agreed to give him a reference.

'When I hear of someone wanting to go to the mission field,' Mr Nash explained, 'I always put a barrier in front of him. There's nothing worse than going to the Mission field uncalled. It doesn't matter what I say. If he is called, the Lord will break that barrier down, as he has with you.'

Alan Belcher arrived in Sabah in September 1940 to help in the building up of a work which had begun three years earlier. At that time the door to the Lun Bawang had been closed. The BEM, as we have seen, was looking for other openings. Hudson Southwell had for some time been concerned for Sabah. He voiced this concern to the conference of missionaries meeting in 1936, and they agreed that God was 'stirring our hearts for British North Borneo'.

Hudson set out with Stafford Young in April 1937 to undertake an exploratory journey right through the heart of the interior of Sabah. They followed the usual route in those days, crossing the Brunei Bay to the island of Labuan and then recrossing the Bay to Weston in Sabah on the northern end of the Bay. From there they took the wood-fired train which followed the 76 miles of railway track to Kota Kinabalu (then known as Jesselton). They joined the branch line at mile 21 at Beaufort which took them up the Padas gorge, cutting through the great Crocker range. Here the traveller must be impressed with the incredible amount of work that had had to be done to hack a railway line out of the side of the mountain, using only hand tools.

In the early days of the railway, 'there were few who cared to risk a long journey without a large basket containing two days' rations', according to Owen Rutter.[1] It was a journey which inspired an anonymous poet to write the famous lines:

> 'Over the metals all rusted brown,
> Thunders the "mail" to Jesselton Town;
> Tearing on madly, recking not Fate,
> Making up time – she's two days late . . .
> See how the sparks from her smoke-stack shower,
> Swaying on wildly at three miles an hour.
> Sometimes they stop to examine a bridge;
> Sometimes they stick on the crest of a ridge . . .'

or sometimes passengers had to get out and walk (as they still do) from one train to another, if a landslide blocked the track.

Passing through the gorge, perhaps the most beautiful part of a very beautiful country, the missionaries arrived at Tenom, a small township on the plain where the two men again studied a map of the area. To the south were the Tagals, totally untouched by the Gospel. They longed to go there but permission was not forthcoming. The

[1] British North Borneo, Owen Rutter, 1922.

openings came to the north, in the vast areas of the large Dusun tribe. Later permission was given to them to set up a work in Ranau in the central highlands of Sabah.

Here Mount Kinabalu, which Hudson described as a 'granite giant two and a half miles high', dominates the scenery for many miles. The clouds hang round it in an endless variety of shapes like a constant change of garments, and it is small wonder that this awe-inspiring mountain took on a mystical role. It dominated the lives of the Dusuns who believed that the spirits of the dead dwelt there. Sacrifices had to be made if anyone dared to assault its upper slopes. Spirits dominated the lives of the Dusuns, just as the other tribes. Although the missionaries found them more sophisticated than the tribes they had met in Sarawak, they were nevertheless affected by the excessive drinking of rice beer which seemed to be such an integral part of Bornean animism.

The Dusuns are much smaller in stature than the Iban, rather more like the Bisayas. They are darker too, also like the Bisayas. The two missionaries observed that they did not build longhouses. Travel too was different. The government had tried to make walking easier for the expatriate by a series of graded bridle tracks (though these are often avoided by the local people. They are necessarily longer, and to those used to walking up and down hills, walking long distances on the comparative flat of a bridle track makes their calf muscles ache!).

Stafford moved in to open up the work in Ranau. To back him up, and also because of the need for a more suitable headquarters where new recruits could be trained and could learn Malay, it was decided to look for a house in Kota Kinabalu. By February 1939 the Southwells moved there, after having been forced by ill-health to leave their house at Nanga Meruyu.

They set up a small Bible School for nine Lun Bawang from the Upper Trusan and were able to give them much-needed teaching for a year. After that the school had to be closed as the Southwells had to go on leave.

When Alan arrived in September 1940 there were therefore no missionaries at Kota Kinabalu, and so he made his way almost directly to Ranau. There, surrounded by Dusuns, he sought to teach himself Malay. His arrival relieved Stafford for overdue leave, and Alan settled down to work with Trevor White who had arrived from England the previous year.

The two young men spent the next year felling trees and building a more permanent house, to which Stafford hoped to bring his new wife. They interspersed their manual labours with language learning and as much travelling as possible to the surrounding hundreds of little Dusun houses and villages.

Working with Trevor and Alan was a young Dusun, Kentuni. One day, while Trevor was out travelling, he came to Alan in great distress.

Kentuni explained his anxiety.

'According to our custom, when you go to sleep, your soul goes walkabout. That doesn't matter. It happens every time you go to sleep. But it is serious if the soul leaves any indications of where it has been. I've just been down to our paddy hut and there was a little heap of paddy on the floor and in it the footprint of one of my children. They haven't been down there. It must be the soul of one of them.'

'What are you going to do?'

'It means calling the witchdoctor. We'll have to kill fowls and have a ceremony to try to placate the spirits. It will be very expensive, but if we succeed the child will not die.'

'There is another way,' Alan tried to explain in his halting Malay. He told him of the victory in Christ who was more powerful than all the spirits. Kentuni decided he would trust Christ. His wife was furious.

'You don't care if our children die,' she screamed at him, but he stuck to his decision.

Unfortunately the next day Alan had arranged to go to see a malarial research doctor, Dr MacArthur, who lived down the bridle track at Tambunan. He prayed anxiously as he travelled and during the next three weeks.

'How are the children?' he asked as soon as he arrived back.

'They are fine,' Kentuni replied. 'We had an enemy. He had put the rice on the floor and taken one of his own children to make the footprint. He did it just to frighten me, it was all a hoax.' Hoax or not, Kentuni knew that the very fear of having offended the spirits had sometimes killed people, and he had proved to himself that Christianity was a better way.

Shortly after this the Japanese landed in Borneo. Trevor decided that Alan and he could stay on at Ranau, but how would they live? There was no large Christian community as in the Trusan where the other missionaries were being supported by the Christians in gratitude for teaching and translation. They would have to support themselves.

Here Alan's contact with Dr John MacArthur developed. Alan was an analytical chemist. John had never done any work on sifting research data and writing a research report, while Alan had, so John suggested he should employ Alan to help him. Trevor did not like the idea of missionaries earning money in this way, but there was really no alternative. Alan supported both himself and Trevor for some months, until being given an ultimatum to surrender. They went to Beaufort but were eventually transferred to Kuching where they were joined at the end of 1942 by the rest of the BEM team from Sarawak.

That was the end of communications from Borneo. There was not a word to break the agonising silence for two years. But they were 'cut off in one sense only', wrote Winsome after the war, 'for we used to realize constantly how lined up we were with you through prayer'. And she went on to detail the awareness they had of the prayers of those at home.

'The first outstanding answer in my mind was a sudden liberation from fear which lasted throughout all those years of war. Above the noise of guns at the coast, and the racket of the motor in the little launch as my husband and I journeyed along the river, the word came clearly, "What are the Japanese to ME?" And when I heard it, I just laughed aloud, so great was the sense of joy and relief.'

The two members of the team who were at home, Stafford Young and Enid Davidson, together with Harold McCracken, President of the Home Council, kept prayer alive in Australia until news of the missionaries' internment reached them at the beginning of 1944 and until they were finally released in September 1945.

Harold had taken over as President in 1935 at a very critical time in the Mission's history. Founded with a modified version of the CIM constitution, the BEM was always intended to be a Field-directed mission. Initially, however, it was agreed that three such young men were not ready to take complete control, and so temporarily control was in the hands of the Home Council.

When those on the field felt strongly that it was time for all major decisions to be taken on the Field, Hudson and Stafford had come home to discuss the future with the Home Council. Mr Nash and some of the older members of the Council had felt that it was still premature and had resigned. Harold McCracken, a young solicitor in practice, found himself President of a very tiny council but, young as he was, he had the wisdom and grace to steer them through the crisis. He was God's man for the occasion and he continued to play a vital part in the establishment of the evangelical church of Borneo.

Through his incredible hard work and considerable self sacrifice he was able to keep the organization at the home end to a minimum. His own secretaries for many years typed the endless letters which he wrote to the field, particularly during the twenty years after the war when he acted as 'fellow labourer, counsellor and friend' to Alan Belcher when Alan was Field Chairman. Indeed his interest, intimate knowledge, penetrating insight and prayerfulness made him as much a part of the scaffolding to God's building in Borneo as any missionary on the field. Harold remained President for 35 years until his retirement in 1971.

In May 1945 Harold and Stafford put out a leaflet entitled *Borneo still calls!* In it they called for friends not to slacken their efforts in prayer for the church and the missionaries now that the Allies were on the advance in the Pacific.

'There is the precedent of one Japanese prison camp in the Philippines where the imminent advance of the Allies meant that the enemy fired and gunned the prisoners . . . we cannot just sit back and say "It cannot happen to our folk".'

But for the sudden cessation of hostilities and a Christian commanding officer, this is exactly what would have happened to the whole band of BEM missionaries. The war ended 15th August 1945. The 17th had been set aside for the annihilation of the Kuching camp.

Plans had been made for a death march for the healthy, followed by the firing of the camp in which would have been left all the sick, the women and the children. When Japan surrendered, the subordinate officers wanted to carry out the plan notwithstanding, but Lt-Col. Suga (who sadly later committed suicide) refused to allow it. He had often attended the services held by the missionaries in the camp and, though conducting the camp on the rigorous lines of discipline demanded by the Japanese, he had tried to keep as much humanity as possible in his dealings with the prisoners and internees. He certainly saved the lives of all in the camp.

After the official surrender, the situation around Kuching nevertheless remained tense for another month as there were 5,000 Japanese in the area and only 500 Australians had landed there. Finally, two jeep loads of Australians drove up to the camp. They were all volunteers, all over 6 feet 2 inches tall. It was a wise strategy. The Japanese are very conscious of their height and when these enormous Australians jumped out of the jeeps, armed to the teeth, the camp surrendered without a shot being fired. All who were still alive were safe.

'I will never forget the excitement of that day,' wrote Winsome. 'The word passed round "put on your best clothes and come up to the square". But no one waited to look for best clothes. For in a few moments we were to hear those words, unbelievable but true, "I now declare you to be free people."'

Free, yes, but what was the future of the BEM? Internment had been costly. One of the outstanding pioneers had died. Frank had had treatment for an ulcer in 1941 but even so enjoyed good health during the rigours of life in the jungle until October 1942, when he and his party surrendered to the Japanese. Poor and inadequate camp food began to affect his health. Suffering himself, he was acutely aware of the problems of others. He initiated special cooking for the sick and during 1943 had done most of that work himself. There had been many answers to prayer for special needs, including some 250 eggs smuggled into the camp. They were kept in bamboos, so that they could be turned regularly. As the bamboos were used for hanging up clothes, they were never discovered by the guards. But gradually Frank's health deteriorated until, just shortly after the first Liberator plane flew over the camp and some four months before the final liberation, Frank died a triumphant death on 27th April

1945. He had continued to work on his translation, making a final revision of Luke's Gospel during 1944, and was the only man in camp who wrote regularly to his wife on two rolls of toilet paper which would take ink. 'His death was a great witness,' Alan Belcher said on looking back. 'Frank had one of these beautiful Penan finely-woven rattan mats which he had used constantly on his travels. We wrapped his body in that and buried him in it.'

There were two casualties of a different sort. The Bewshers resigned.

'I lost my faith in 1943 while in internment,' Ro Bewsher explained recently. 'It was as a result of association with German Jewish refugee doctors with whom I worked as a gardener, and I was not restored to faith until 1958 when I was in England.' Ro returned to Borneo in 1947 to work in the Agricultural Department in Sarawak. He went on to say, sadly but graciously, 'I am happy to say that my relationship with the Mission has been good throughout, but I continue to regret my defection and to regard with envy and admiration the continued service of my contemporaries who kept their hand to the plough and brought such fruit for eternity.'

With the loss of three such valued workers and with five others having suffered the rigours of internment and needing a rest, there were those who thought the BEM was finished. How could such an infant church have survived three years of isolation? The work would have to start all over again.

But God was again underlining his statement that 'I will build my church and the gates of hell shall not prevail against it'. It was His church, His building. He had again been working while the missionaries were cut off. And He was calling five young ex-servicemen as well as some single ladies who would more than double the ranks of the little team and witness wonderful new advances for the Gospel in Borneo.

CHAPTER 8

THE LIGHT SPREADS

'SOLDIERS!' – the word went round the Chinese family in hiding in a remote little farmstead in Labuan. The war was only just over and there was still fear and suspicion everywhere. There were quite a few Japanese not yet rounded up and you could not be too careful.

Only the father remained to face the intruders. Tall and dignified, Chin Tsun Leong was trembling as he went to meet them, even though they were unarmed.

'Are you Mr Chin Tsun Leong?' the soldiers enquired.

'Yes, gentlemen, can I help you?' he managed to say in his immaculate English with the courtesy of the East and a poise which he always showed, whatever his feelings

'We're Christians,' they said, 'and we have been told that you are too. We've been looking all over the island for you.'

'Welcome, gentlemen, you are doubly welcome! Yes, we have been in hiding. No one quite knows what is happening on the island at present. Excuse me a moment.'

With the characteristic clap of his hands, he called something in Chinese. Children appeared from all over the place. One, two, three, still they came, down to the tiniest of all with their mother. Eight of them, nervous, shy and silent.

A few more words from Leong, and then the children began to sing, sweet voices singing hymns to tell the soldiers, 'Yes, we are Christians too.'

No one at the time knew it, but this was the beginning of a close friendship with one of those soldiers, Ray Cunningham, and also the beginning of many happy years of sharing with the BEM in the building of the church in Borneo. Leong made regular visits to Lawas to minister to the little groups of Chinese Christians, until he went to be with his Lord in 1970.

Twelve months after this encounter, Hudson Southwell returned to Labuan in August 1946 to recommence the work begun before the war. Barely a year had elapsed since he and his fellow missionaries had spent a few happy weeks on that beautiful little island. They had been recuperating from internment before being flown home. Barely a year, but Hudson could be restrained no longer. He had to get back to see how the infant church had survived the war years.

'Desolation and confusion meet the eye everywhere,' he wrote on arrival. 'Trees gnarled and torn; palms blasted and decapitated, buildings razed to rubble, rusty pontoons and barges along the beach; while here and there atap thatch shanties are springing up. . . .'

Hudson was not on the island long before he too had an encounter with Chin Tsun Leong. Why had he come alone? Leong, always polite, but nevertheless forthright, sent a message through Hudson to the people of Australia.

'Tell the people of Australia how much we need more young men as missionaries. I cannot understand why more of these young men who have seen the need as soldiers, are not returning as missionaries.'

In fact God was calling Ray Cunningham and others, but neither Hudson nor Leong knew it at the time.

Hudson felt very much alone. Added to the picture of general desolation was a more personal loss. He did not yet know that on the mainland the BEM had lost everything – buildings, furniture, boats, books, typewriters, clothes and most personal effects, including valuable language data which Ro Bewsher had buried while in hiding from the Japanese. What he did know was the loss through looting of a vast amount of equipment given by the liberating forces. It had been set aside for them when they had passed through Labuan, so that they

82

could re-establish the work when they returned. Hardly a vestige of it remained.

Materially the picture was black, but the future was not.

Hudson crossed to the mainland of Sarawak by the regular launch service to the tiny township of Lawas, two hours upriver from the coast. On September 1st he met with the Lun Bawang Christians in their little church. Two hundred believers were crammed inside. Just nearby was the charred remains of the church which they had built during the war and which had been burnt down by the Japanese. The old, black and charred; the new, teeming with life. The church was ready for a new beginning, as was the whole of Borneo.

It was the same story in Sabah. Trevor White and Stafford Young returned in September, Stafford being mainly concerned to see if light aircraft could be used to speed up movement in the interior of Borneo. Ranau had been the end of the death march from Sandakan on which so many of the Australian Eighth Division had lost their lives. The Dusuns had fled to the hills but had come back to build a church right on the spot where the forty survivors of the march had been shot. Before the war just a few here and there were interested, and now many hundreds were meeting for worship. This was in spite of the fact that many thought the missionaries would never return and some thought they were dead.

Kentuni was there. He had not changed his mind since that moment of putting Jesus Christ to the test, and he had done what he continued to do for many years to come. He had travelled and talked of what he knew, and he had quite a group around him, waiting to commit themselves to the new Christian way. Trevor found himself visiting many of the 25 villages surrounding Ranau on weekdays and returning on Sundays to share in the central services. During the first year alone, four hundred were baptized and a group of men set aside for training as leaders.

Leaders – that was the need of the Lun Bawang too. Hudson decided that a Bible school was top priority and that this should be at Lawas, together with the new headquarters of the BEM. It was easy of access for the Lun Bawang and others from the interior, and the regular launch service made it easy of access from the coast. This was understandably a great shock and disappointment to the Lun Bawang of the lower Trusan who assumed that the Mission would rebuild the base which the Davidsons had had there before the war, but Hudson was looking to the future. He expected that soon other tribes would be joining the Lun Bawang for training.

Hudson worked on getting buildings up quickly with the willing help of the local Lun Bawang. The hill site at Budok Ngeri which was allocated to the Mission was dominated by three towering trees. Under the old customs, they were feared as the home of the spirits. How fitting it was that here the future leaders of the church should be trained, demonstrating daily that they were no longer gripped by the fear and domination of the spirits.

The school was opened in April 1947 with Brian Morcombe in charge; he was assisted at first by Winsome Southwell, then later by Enid Davidson and Madge Belcher. Brian had been with Frank during those early months of Japanese occupation of Borneo and he had seen the way Frank had selected key couples from each village, so that they could return to their villages as leaders. He had also seen the C and MA work when Frank and he had made a visit to Indonesia during those months.

'It seemed to me,' Brian wrote, 'that the C and MA work which was based upon feeder Bible Schools and the Advanced Bible School at Macassar had made remarkable headway by delegation of missionary responsibility to trained pastors and teachers.'

This, of course, had been the aim of the BEM from the very beginning. Efforts had been made both in the

Limbang and at Kota Kinabalu to train local leadership. But it was not until God had worked sovereignly amongst the Lun Bawang that there had been many suitable candidates for training.

All the first students of the Bible School were Lun Bawang, ten couples in all. Many of these had been at Frank's schools and among them was Racha Umong who twelve years later would be the Chairman of the newly-formed Sidang Injil Borneo. Support came mainly from their own people. At Easter 1948 between five and six hundred Lun Bawang gathered for a conference at Lawas, and this number included 68 out of the 75 church leaders. Some of them had walked for ten days to be there. They decided on the principle of tithing their rice crop and cash, and half of what they collected was to be set aside for the new Bible School.

Nevertheless, the students made a small 'garden' near the school to supplement their supplies. There on the hill at Budok Ngeri the jungle was very close. While everyone was in school it was not uncommon for monkeys to take advantage of the situation to look for an easy meal in the garden. Brian soon decided to keep a ·303 rifle in the school room. Anyone with quick eyes and slight lack of concentration would shout, 'Tuan, kuyad!' (Sir, monkeys) and Brian would shoot from the classroom. This saved the crop and·added a little welcome protein to the diet, as well as providing a welcome break from study to those who were more used to hunting than reading.

Hudson, as well as being Field leader, travelled endlessly in those first few years and saw well over 550 Lun Bawang baptised in two years. His first trip, just a few weeks after his arrival, was to the upriver Lun Bawang whom he found standing firm. Those who had been taught during the ten vital months before internment had been able to hold regular meetings for worship, had shared their faith with others and to a large extent had held the church together during the war years. They had also been helped by two teachers sent over from Indonesia by Guru Aris, the leader of the C and MA work there. The BEM Newsletter of November 1946 reports, 'where these two have been stationed the spiritual tone of the Christians has been maintained at a high level'.

Hudson set off again in April 1947, through Lun Bawang country and on to the Kelabits whom he had not seen since he and Frank had visited them in 1940. He found them vastly different. Shortly after that visit, and impressed by what they had seen of the Lun Bawang on both sides of the border, they had sent three of their young men to train in the C and MA school in Belawit, just over the border in Indonesia. These three had then taught their own people, and Guru Aris and some Lun Bawang Christians had also come across to teach. Many had burnt their skulls, charms and fetishes at that time but, as they explained to Hudson, they had maintained the 'social practices' associated with their old custom. They were still drinking heavily.

Guru Paul, a Macassar-trained teacher who still lives in Bario, had also come over during the war and he had had to contend with this heavy drinking. He taught the children in school during the day, and then at night and in the early morning he was able to teach the Christian faith to the older people. Guru Paul, greying slightly, is a small, energetic man with a sparkling sense of humour. His bright, dancing eyes light up his whole face when he talks.

'The people burnt all their skulls but used to pray to God before they drank themselves happily drunk,' he explained. 'I used to teach them in between drinking bouts while they were still just about sober enough to listen.' Then he added, in his philosophical way, 'They may not have gone very far, but they had made a start anyway.'

News of the radical change in the Lun Bawang and the somewhat lesser but nevertheless real change in the

Kelabits, reached the great Baram river as Kelabits passed through villages on their way to the coast. Here was the home of the river-dwelling Kayan and Kenya people, strong, vigorous, able and very deeply entrenched in their old custom. Indeed, the government wanted to see them preserved in their old ways.

But a transformation of such an extraordinary nature to the despised Lun Bawang merited investigation, and one of the most important Kenya chiefs in the area had sent messages to Hudson to come and teach them this new way of life. Hudson was in fact on his way to the Baram, but he was travelling and the message never reached him. Impatient for change, the Penghulu had sent downriver to the Catholics who had had schools and a work in downriver areas for many decades. One month before Hudson arrived the village had become Catholic, and for the next few years the whole situation was very complex.

Hudson reached the Baram from the Kelabit Highlands, by the route of Long Lellang and the Akah river, and he felt that this had been God's leading when he saw the response from the Kayans in the Akah. The journey was no easy one. Starting off down the beautiful Akah river with its lovely overhanging trees, he soon reached a wild wilderness, where the Akah falls into a waterfall. This fall marks the division between Kelabit and Kayan country, and so the Kelabits sent messages for the Kayans to come and collect Hudson. They left him with one Lun Bawang companion, in a little hut at the top of the waterfall, in this most remote part of the jungle. Fortunately the Kayans received the message and hurried to meet them, but the headman was furious that these visitors had been left alone. It was a two-mile walk to where the Kayans had left their boats at the bottom of the fall, and then they went on down the wild rapids of the Akah, where the boat was buffeted and tossed from rock to rock by the rushing water.

It was a great event to have a white man visit these two

BARAM RIVER AREA

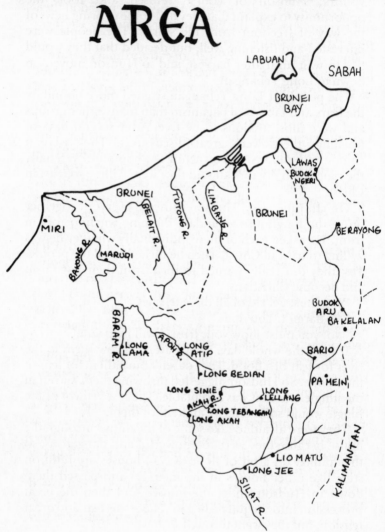

isolated villages and at the first, Long Sinie, one of the witch doctors offered to call down the spirits for the visitors. Hudson of course refused and took the opportunity to explain that they had come to bring news of the way of freedom from the spirits. The people were interested and listening well, but decided that they would like to wait until after harvest, and so Hudson moved on down to Long Tebangan.

The people at Long Tebangan seemed more bound by the fears and taboos of paganism than many other groups and were most anxious to be free. After several days of teaching, there were great discussions. They were a community and insisted on acting as a community. Finally the nine witch doctors all said they were willing to trust in Christ.

On 5th June 1947, Hudson gathered everyone together on to the longhouse verandah, the nine witchdoctors in front. He asked each of these individually whether he was willing to trust in Christ. Then he turned to all the people. Yes, they too really wanted to turn from their paganism and become Christians.

'You must get rid of all these fetishes.'

'We daren't. You do it.'

'No, you must show your trust. I will help you.'

It took the whole day. They daren't throw them in the river for fear of a flood. They daren't burn them for fear of the smoke. So Hudson suggested throwing them far out in the jungle and that was acceptable. The fast growth of the jungle would soon remove all trace of them.

They were afraid to take some of the things through the house because they were too powerful and dangerous, so they pulled up a bit of floor (Kayan houses are built on stilts like other houses in the interior) and passed them down to Hudson under the house. And then the great procession into the jungle began. There was fear and great tension, but they went through with it.

Only on the return journey did the load lighten. Suddenly they began to call out, 'Lord Jesus, we are trusting you only now.' As they climbed back into the longhouse they broke out into spontaneous dancing and singing all down the long verandah.

'The only way I can describe it,' Hudson said later, 'is that a fog seemed to have lifted. I was not expecting anything like it. But it was a wonderful sensation.'

To celebrate their new freedom they decided to go hunting. Fear immediately gripped them again when the first animal they saw was a barking deer, previously a powerful messenger from the spirits and never shot or eaten by them.

'But we are trusting Jesus now,' they shouted and followed it to kill it. It ran into their cemetery – place of even greater fear and dread into which no one would dare go without the necessary sacrifices to the spirits.

'We are trusting Jesus now. The spirits cannot harm us.' They prayed for protection and caught the deer.

What a feast there was that night. It seemed they had had double proof of the reality of what they had done as they ate the previously forbidden food which they had killed in a forbidden place.

These were momentous days. Age-long oppression and fears turned overnight to freedom and rejoicing. It was a mighty step of faith. But had everyone become a true heart-believer? They had certainly experienced the power of Christ to release them from the power of the spirits. Hudson later described it as 'mass conversion with regeneration in some and leading to regeneration in others'. Hudson had to move on to the many others calling for initial teaching, but he must leave them with at least something which could remind them of the ability of the Lord to keep them. In spite of limited Kayan after only three weeks of trying to learn their language, he was able to translate a hymn which has been sung up and down the Baram ever since:

> The strife is o'er, the battle done
> Now is the Victor's triumph won;
> O let the song of praise be sung, Alleluyah.
> Lord, by the stripes which wounded Thee
> From death's dread sting Thy servants free
> That we may live and sing to Thee, Alleluyah.

The work in the Baram had begun. Hudson went on down the tumbling, boiling rapids of the Akah to its junction with the main Baram river. There he met the Kenya Penghulu who had recently become a Catholic. Hudson sadly agreed not to go to the Kenya villages under his jurisdiction as he made his way up the main Baram to another Penghulu's domain. This man, Mape Arang, never became a Christian himself, but was more than happy for Hudson to go to any of his people, many of whom wanted to become Christians.

At Lio Matu in particular, where Kelabits often stayed as they travelled to the coast, many of the Kenya people had seen the change in these Kelabits. They wanted to turn to Christianity, but the witchdoctors, led by one particularly strong and powerful man, were very resistant. One day, when all the people were gathered on the long verandah, Hudson was explaining again this new way of life. The atmosphere was particularly tense with this one witchdoctor very resistant. But as Hudson went on to explain yet again the power of the Lord Jesus to bring freedom from the spirits, this man suddenly jumped up.

'I will yield to the Lord Jesus,' he shouted and immediately others sprang to their feet all over the house. The whole village decided to become Christian.

Then began the tense, tiring, but joyful destruction of their fetishes. Every witchdoctor had a special little receptacle called a *kaulit*. This consisted of nine little cylinders, one inside the other, and inside the smallest of them all was a bead. This was the seat of the spirit. These receptacles were so sacred and so powerful that no woman had ever dared to touch one: Hudson insisted that they be opened up before being thrown out, to show the whole house that the power was gone from them.

Sweating with fear as well as exertion, the Kenya men hacked down the great tall images, great poles which represented the spirits, and they came crashing to the ground. An unusual sight was a great crocodile built of stones at the end of the longhouse. It was a particularly potent charm which had been made by the people, to assist them against the dreaded Japanese. That too was destroyed, and the Kenyas broke out into beautiful singing.

Hudson described it as a particularly awe-inspiring sight, as these men and women threw out all these huge and small symbols of the power of the spirits, which had held them bound for centuries.

God was working among the Kayans as well as among the Kenyas. In January 1948 Alan and Madge Belcher, who had arrived with Enid Davidson in July 1947, set off for the Baram to spend four months in visiting and teaching, much of the time being spent at Long Tebangan. It was hoped to set up a base and a school there, as the whole Baram area was crying out for education. They made arrangements for the building of a school and the Kayans chose a site for a mission house.

The Belchers also went up to Long Sinie where the people had promised to 'turn' after harvest. There was strong opposition and only the headman and three other families were determined enough to turn to Christianity. The others wanted to but feared the opposition, and a tense situation continued for some time. The Southwells visited their Penghulu who lived quite a long way away in the Apoh river and he was at first friendly, but later became violently opposed. Nevertheless, despite many hours of arguments and discussions, when the Southwells visited Long Sinie later in the year the people eventually all turned to Christianity. Winsome Southwell described one lovely aspect of their new-found faith.

'The Kayans' life is full of restrictions and taboos on every action and before these taboos could be broken they felt their need of specific prayer. Thus it was that the women came for special prayer about their children. Up to a certain age, a baby is never taken . . . outside on to the river's edge until a sacrificial offering is made to the spirits. But now boldly and in faith in the power of the Lord Jesus, they asked that I would conduct them to the river . . . some (of the children) were very dirty and sooty from the fireplace and we all joined in scrubbing.' The women were prepared to trust their most precious possessions to their new-found Saviour.

There were many and varied political undercurrents to the whole advance into the Baram area. On one visit the Southwells called to see the Resident in Miri. He admitted frankly that, although a Protestant himself, he wanted to leave the Baram exclusively for the Catholics to simplify administration. But he had been overridden by the Governor of Sarawak and the Supreme Council. This was after the Governor's visit to Lawas in November 1947. He had come with the Rt Hon. Malcolm MacDonald, then Governor-General of Malaya and British Borneo, to present medals to the Lun Bawang and Kelabits for their contribution to the paratroopers dropped into the interior during the war. The two Governors had taken the opportunity of visiting the school and mission station at Budok Ngeri and had been impressed with what had been achieved.

The next big advance in the Baram came, remarkably, through the Penghulu who had so opposed the turning of Long Sinie to Christianity. By February 1949, this very

Penghulu was asking the Southwells to go to his village of Long Atip in the Apoh river, as he wanted all under his jurisdiction to become Christians. They had seen the difference in those who had 'turned'.

'The joy is great, but the responsibility is tremendous', Hudson wrote as they set off overland from the Akah. They were amazed by the situation which awaited them. The Penghulu, thoroughly opposed to them a year before, welcomed them most warmly, but initially the villagers were suspicious. However, after several days of teaching, they too became enthusiastic and it was not long before they had all agreed to become Christians and the long process of throwing out of fetishes had begun.

'Probably one of the most helpful factors was the happy and spontaneous witnessing of the Long Tebangan people who accompanied us,' was the significant comment which Hudson made later. Again, it was Borneans witnessing to Borneans. Hudson continued,

'God has done wonderful things which seemed impossible a few months ago. Three large Kayan villages and the majority of another village have turned to Christ and cast out all their pagan fetishes and emblems, so that 1,067 more Kayans are now trusting the Lord Jesus.'

This incredible openness was the main impression on Horrie Hamer when he arrived in the Baram shortly after reaching Borneo with fellow ex-servicemen Ken Cooper and Sam Gollan in October 1948.

'Both Kayans and Kenyas are in a strangely responsive attitude towards the Gospel,' he wrote. 'I say strangely, because surely there are few places where such opportunities abound for telling the message of salvation to communities so ready to receive it.'

These three men were most welcome additions to the hard-pressed team, Ken going with Horrie to open the school and do considerable medical work at Long Tebangan while Sam went to help Trevor White who was

Kenya children

still a lone figure amidst the endless calls for teaching in Sabah. Still further additions came the following year when Mr Chin Tsun Leong really began to see the answer to his Macedonian call. Ex-sapper Ray Cunningham arrived, accompanied by ex-fighter pilot Bruce Morton who had flown over Borneo during the war. They brought with them the little Aeronca aircraft given by Stafford Young which heralded a new phase of the BEM's history.

* * * * *

The period 1938–1950 had been an exciting one. There is almost a sense of breathlessness as one sees God taking the initiative in bringing thousands into the Church – Lun Bawang, Kelabits, Kayans, Kenyas, Dusuns. In addition there had been further contact with the wandering Penans who were clamouring for teaching, and the occasional contact with the Tagals indicated that they would welcome the Christian message. There was still room for endless travelling into new areas but there was also a great need for teaching these thousands of young Christians.

To meet these new needs the BEM team, though larger, was once again young and inexperienced. In addition to the five young ex-servicemen, the Mission had been able for the first time to welcome single ladies into its ranks. Nurse Win Burrow, and Jean Harris who was soon to be married to Sam Gollan, arrived in 1948. Win did considerable medical work at Lawas while learning Malay, before going to join the Southwells who had begun to build up the new work at Long Atip. During the following two years four more young ladies had arrived, Leah Cubit and Dorothy Summerson, together with the fiancées of Ken Cooper and Horrie Hamer.

Only five of the pre-war team were left by 1950 and two of these, Trevor White and Alan Belcher, had had very little time in Borneo before being interned. The Morcombes had had to return to Australia during 1948 due to ill-health and Enid Davidson was just about to go on leave to find that family responsibilities for her two fatherless children would keep her at home. The only experienced missionaries were the Southwells.

The team had changed and the leadership had also changed. At the 1948 Conference Hudson Southwell, whose energetic enthusiasm had led the Mission through twenty years of sometimes hard and sometimes exciting pioneering, was succeeded by a man many years his junior. Hudson continued to serve on the Mission Executive but Alan Belcher was to lead the team through the fifties and sixties.

PART 3

HOW SHORT IS THE DAY?

1950–1970

Tribal dancing

CHAPTER 9

INDEPENDENCE

'THE first thing you are to do is to start working yourself out of a job,' was the advice given by Bishop Alf Stanway of Tanganyika to one of his new recruits.

After discussions in Melbourne in 1950 the BEM Home Council suggested to the Field Conference that they should consider the possibility of working towards specific withdrawal. As a later BEM publication put it,

'It is unthinkable that any constructor would produce a house propped up by scaffolding. What a house it would be if it began to totter as he removed what was meant to be a temporary aid to construction. By definition missions are temporary affairs. . . . If we are not constantly planning our withdrawal even in our latest advances, we are on dangerous ground. We may be running ourselves into situations that would prove very embarrassing to the building of the church which we trust God will establish.'

Of course BEM had always been a mission with a strong emphasis on the indigenous church. The small Bisaya church had run its own affairs. The Lun Bawang had been left during the war years with a local leader in each group and they had taken the Gospel to the Kelabits. The Dusuns were already doing much of the evangelism themselves as well as running their own church organization, and of course the same applied to the more recent advances in the Baram. The Bible School at Lawas was training local people to take over the leadership and a number of students had already accompanied the missionaries on evangelistic trips to tribes other than their own.

The Home Council suggested ten years. The Field

Conference met in August 1950 to consider the proposal. They were very aware that they were mostly young and inexperienced and many were still at the language learning stage. Lack of personnel and consequent lack of teaching was beginning to lead to a serious problem of nominalism in the churches. There was a great ignorance of the Scriptures – in fact most had no Scriptures in their languages. In the Baram, the Bungan cult had arisen and become very popular. This was a moderated form of paganism in which the penalties and taboos were greatly reduced and which was therefore very acceptable to those who had seen the breaking of the bondage of fear among the Christians.

The team was hard pressed. No resident missionary could be spared for the Kelabits nor for any part of the Limbang, and the Tagals were still a great untouched field. Even where the churches were established, the missionaries could not forget that former illiterate, ignorant, drunken tribesmen were the raw material and that the aim was the building of a church as nearly as possible like that of which we read in the Acts of the Apostles.

Against such a background, it was an audacious plan. But as the Conference considered it, they began to believe that it was God's plan for the Mission. They agreed in principle, but felt fifteen years was a more realistic figure, especially remembering the number of New Testaments which would need to be translated.

The fifteen-year policy was adopted and Harold McCracken summed up the situation after the conference.

'The remarkable visitation of God's Spirit, coupled with the urgent political situation which might shut the door to missionary work in South-East Asia and the possibility of the soon coming return of the Lord, led the Mission to the conviction that it was God's will that we should aim to complete our task in fifteen years. By that time the Mission aimed to have a church in Borneo which would be sufficiently grounded and instructed to be able to take over the responsibility of the Christian witness and evangelization of the still-untouched tribes. This would mean, on the part of the field, a more intensive programme of evangelism than ever before.'

He went on to point out that it would be necessary to have an increase of missionaries together with the intensive training of the leaders of the future church. It would also mean that at home there would have to be 'an increased measure of sacrifice', and he urged the friends of the Mission to 'pray harder and give more sacrificially than ever before'.

A specific item for prayer was to be for twelve new workers in the next twelve months – an increase of 70 per cent in the size of the team.[1]

Fifteen years was not very long. But did the Mission have even that long? And what about the increasing nominalism in the churches?

The missionary exodus from China in 1950 had forced two questions on Alan Belcher's mind as he visited and taught the Lun Bawang churches. Would they stand if the missionaries had to withdraw, not for just three years as during the war, but indefinitely as from China? Secondly, would the Lun Bawang Christians endure in the face of persecution?

Alan and Madge set themselves to pray daily and when they came to the Conference in 1952 God had already begun to do a new work in their own hearts and lives. In addition God had already answered that prayer for twelve new workers, most of whom had reached Borneo in time for the Conference, the remaining three coming shortly afterwards.

[1] Over the next decade the Mission increased to over fifty members. Many names could be mentioned but, with the increased emphasis on the Bornean members of the church, it seems fitting to keep the missionaries rather more in the background from 1950 onwards.

During and after the conference, God worked remarkably in many of the missionary team. Oswald Sanders, who as General Director of the OMF had visited Borneo in 1956, wrote in his Foreword to *Jungle Fire*, 'A great leap forward in the work took place in 1952 as the outcome of a sovereign moving of the Holy Spirit among the missionaries. They discovered anew that spiritual success comes only when the Holy Spirit is able to work unhindered by carnality and sin in His chosen instruments. With confession and cleansing came new vision, this time of long-range planning to be implemented with short-term urgency.'

It began to look more possible to implement the decision to establish a church and move the scaffolding on.

Immediately after the conference a Lun Bawang pastor, Sigar Berauk, was the first tribal pastor to conduct the communion service. This was held in the Lawas church with Bible School students and missionaries attending.

The blessing which was changing the lives of the missionary team spread into the Bible School, where Madge Belcher was now Principal. Singa Achang, one of Frank Davidson's school students in the pre-war days, had returned to school for a refresher course and was head student. On 25th August 1952 his little three-year-old son, Pengiran, was drowned. The grief of the parents following this tragedy was used by God to soften the hearts of all the Bible School students. Conviction of sin led to a great hunger for the Lord and a deepening of spiritual life.

The blessing spread to the pastors. On Monday, September 8th, thirteen pastors, including two wives, came to a pastors' conference at Lawas. They came together for Bible study and to share and discuss their problems for the future.

'It seemed to us that these much-loved and faithful pastors would have little to confess, but we prayed for a movement of God's Spirit among them, because God had shown some of us missionaries our need of revival,' wrote Madge Belcher, describing the conference. 'We testified to them of the blessing of the Holy Spirit in our own lives. We confessed to them our own failures in the past. We told of the wonderful cleansing Blood of Jesus and the filling of the Holy Spirit, and the consequent victory over sin and the love and joy and peace that God had given.'

By the second day of the conference, all the pastors and their wives had come under conviction of sin as they came together in heartfelt prayer. God gave His blessing to that little gathering which was the embryo from which would develop the Inter-Tribal Conference of the *Sidang Injil Borneo* (the Evangelical Church of Borneo).

The pastors began to meet yearly and by December 1954 a representative body was formed for the administration of church affairs. It comprised representatives of six tribal churches (Lun Bawang, Kayan, Kenya, Dusun, Kelabit and Tagal) together with Racha Umong and Udan Rangat, a Lun Bawang who had graduated from Bible School and then joined the staff. The BEM was represented by the Belchers.

The following year, 1955, over ninety pastors and their wives came together and the little Bisaya church was represented for the first time. Then in 1956 all meetings were chaired by Racha Umong. Udan was the Secretary and Alan Belcher was asked 'to join the council as adviser and liaison between the church and missionary body'.

Finally in 1959, the Conference was ready to draw up a constitution for the evangelical church in Borneo. At this conference they were helped by representatives from KINGME, the evangelical church founded in Indonesia by the Christian and Missionary Alliance. This part of God's building was taking shape and *Sidang Injil Borneo* was chosen as its official name. Racha continued as Chairman with Sigar Berauk as his deputy. Udan was getting ready to go to Australia for further training and his place was taken by another Lun Bawang, Kelasi Ating. For the first time a Kayan, Juk Wan, joined the Executive.

The SIB was now an independent church, just a few years before Independence came to Borneo. On 31st August 1963 the Borneo States became part of the new Federation of Malaysia.

With Independence came the need for elections. Political parties were formed and a new word was introduced to the languages of these tribal peoples who, for centuries, had lived as united but isolated communities under their elders and tribal chiefs.

Politics had an effect on the church which was somewhat unexpected from the Western point of view. The only contact that the interior tribespeople had with the outside world was when travelling to the coast for trade, when world affairs would hardly touch them. There were no transistor radios or newspapers in the far interior. Frequently the person in the village most aware of national affairs would be the pastor and his education stood him in good stead to represent the people in Government. To the Western missionaries it was somewhat disturbing to find that pastors began to be pressed to stand for parliament.

It was a particular shock to their preconceived western ideas, when the SIB leaders at Lawas said that they were going to nominate Racha for local government. Racha, an ex-headman, was born for leadership, but would not this be an unwise precedent? The SIB graciously pointed out two factors which did not apply in the home countries of the missionaries. Although religious freedom was written into the constitution of Malaysia, it would nevertheless be good to have a strong Christian voice in a position of influence. Secondly, only pastors and church leaders, apart from government teachers, had adequate education and experience to make a positive contribution. There were no laymen. The missionaries had to agree it was a wise move.

*   *   *   *   *

While the SIB was developing its independent organization, the fifteen-year policy was greatly stimulating the missionaries to give high priority to teaching this emerging church at all levels. At the grass-roots level there was an extensive programme of teaching in short-term village schools, deacons' schools and conventions. There were short-term pastors' schools and conferences in some areas as well as the training of future pastors. Central to the whole programme was the continued development of the Bible School, together with the establishment of Feeder Bible Schools in different areas.

The Bible School at Lawas had quickly outgrown the site at Budok Ngeri. By 1950 it was moved downriver, together with the Headquarters of the BEM, to a new site nearer the Lawas township. The land had been given by the Lawas Rubber Company, fifteen acres of flat land on which no rubber had been planted. There was room for Bible school buildings, dormitories, offices, homes for missionaries, and an area where wet rice fields could provide for some of the needs of the students. This time the project was not the sole responsibility of the local Lun Bawang. Trevor White left the pressing needs in the Ranau area and took a team of Dusun Christians to spend three months helping with the initial large building programme.

It was among the Dusuns that the first deacons' schools were held. Trevor had for some time been concerned to set up a school for the training of deacons, so that they would be better equipped to teach in their villages. The constant calls from many villages for teaching and preaching had however kept him in his travelling ministry. Just before he went to Lawas the Gollans, therefore, set up the first deacons' school on 1st March 1950, while they were still learning the language. Most of the deacons and a number of young men who were potential leaders used to come in for training four days a week, returning to their villages at weekends. They would pass on what they had learnt, and calls soon began to come from other villages for them to visit.

Kentuni was one of these men. He and another younger man, Kerangkas, travelled endlessly and the church began to see its responsibility to help them financially and with their farms. God put His seal on the ministry of these men by many answers to prayer, some of them quite remarkable.

One evening, Kentuni had planned to hold a service. The people had already gathered in the house when an exceptionally severe thunderstorm broke. Two pagan women were present and were so afraid of the storm that they could not sit still and didn't know where to hide themselves. Kentuni led in prayer about the storm and the planned services. He thanked God for His mighty power over all things and committed the situation to Him. With dramatic suddenness the storm ceased. There was not another rumble of thunder to interfere with the meeting. One of the pagan women gave her heart to the Lord.

Many of the 15,000 Dusuns living in close proximity to Ranau were scattered on mountain ridges, and teaching them involved considerable travelling, as Trevor had discovered. By 1957 a system of rather more consecutive teaching, involving a more economical use of travelling time, was begun. By this time Trevor had resigned from the Mission and had begun a new work in the Kota Belud area. Teaching teams began to go to a village for a month to give concentrated teaching and it was hoped that, by covering key villages, the Word would spread out to others. A development of these short-term schools came in 1963 when the Dusun field was divided into five areas and groups of about 25 pastors and deacons met together to study the Bible and to share problems and fellowship. Similar schools were begun for pastors in Tagal country in

1964, where the pastors were particularly aware of their isolation and need for teaching.

Deacons' schools had also become a vital part of the year's calendar in the Sarawak tribes, where the yearly convention became the other major event. In their old custom these tribes had been used to considerable gatherings for feasts, and the Christians soon adapted these gatherings to the idea of a Christian convention. This started in 1948 among the Lun Bawang, and by 1955 the first really inter-tribal convention took place at Pa Mein in the Kelabit Highlands. A village of 150 people entertained 1,200 Kayans, Kenyas, Lun Bawang and Penans, with even a few from the small Saban tribe from the Upper Baram. The Highlands are fertile and thanks to the help of surrounding villages, everyone had enough and there was even some rice left over.

The Baram visitors were particularly amazed at what they experienced.

'We couldn't have met like this in the old days. Someone would have got hurt,' said a leading Kenya deacon who was greatly encouraged to see that there were so many Christians.

The smooth organization for feeding such a large crowd was mainly thanks to Guru Paul, the first government teacher mentioned earlier, and to Mein Ribu, a deacon from Pa Mein.

Mein Ribu was one of the first Kelabits to become a Christian. Three years later, such was his hunger for the Lord that, when missionaries visited the Kelabit Highlands, he followed them from village to village for a month in order to get more teaching.

'What is the use of having plenty of rice and cattle, if I die without knowing the Word of God?' he had said.

The next year, 1952, he had walked for two weeks to attend a Lun Bawang deacons' school and he and the Lun

Bawang deacons had been 'caught up in the same fire as the Bible School students and missionaries'. Mein Ribu had returned to pray for and teach his relatives and friends for the three years prior to this great gathering which he had helped to organize. Though there was great blessing at the convention, a missionary noticed that no one came from Mein Ribu's village for counselling. The explanation lay in the fact that he had been in his home church every morning, pouring out his heart to God on behalf of his village. They had come to repentance and blessing before the convention.

On these special occasions the church members were being built up, but the day-to-day teaching was done by the pastor in each village. More and more villages were calling for pastors, and the numbers of students in training at the central Bible school had increased by 1962 to 170. That year the Lun Bawang decided it was time they had their own feeder Bible school, and so they all contributed and built the Budok Aru school near Ba Kelalan.

Before the school could be opened on 27th June 1963, Confrontation with Indonesia had turned the quiet, peaceful border area into a danger zone, but they went ahead.

'I must admit I'm frightened at times,' said the principal, but over and above the sense of danger a real peace pervaded the school when Madge Belcher visited them in October of that year to help them plan the curriculum. In spite of continuous reports of enemy activity, new students kept enrolling and there were soon 74, not just Lun Bawang but also Kelabits, Kayans, Dusuns and Penans. They continuously experienced the Lord's protection. In fact both military and civil authorities expressed surprise that the Ba Kelalan area had not had more raids.

Two years later, two more feeder Bible schools were established. One was at Long Bedian in the Apoh, for

Penans and Kayans. This was a development from a small Penan school begun earlier. The other school was in Sabah for the Dusuns. Nemaus was nine and a half miles over a rough jeep track from Ranau and the school was opened with 23 students. The principal was a Dusun who had had experience at Budok Aru after graduating from Lawas.

* * * * *

Perhaps the most significant of all the great steps forward in the development of the SIB during this period was the number of those who became missionaries to other tribes. The first of these were Lun Bawang.

Upai Baru, the man with the biggest smile in Borneo, was the first to go. He went for a few months in October 1951 to team up with Ray Cunningham in his extensive travelling and teaching ministry in the Upper Baram. Then the following year Udan Rangat and his wife Iki went to Ranau and Balang Selutan and Muring went to Long Atip.

Udan was described as 'one of the most outstanding students in the Bible School'. His father, one of the more prosperous of the Lawas Lun Bawang, had a rubber garden and some buffalo as well as a good rice farm. His father-in-law was the Penghulu who was keen for Udan to take over his office at a later date. He was, however, out of sympathy with the Christian message and frequently made life very difficult for Udan and Iki. Once he threatened to disinherit them, but at last he relented and reluctantly allowed them to go to the Dusuns.

Balang was an older man. He had been trained by the C and MA school in Indonesia and was a pastor during the war. In fact it was remarkable that he was alive after the war, as he had sheltered a British airman whom he discovered to be a Christian. The language barrier had been total, but they had been able to communicate their position by each holding up a New Testament. When questioned later at gun point by the Japanese, Balang had pointed out that it was Lun Bawang custom to entertain anyone who called at their houses. They had fed him and sent him on his way.

'I think it was my honesty that saved my life,' Balang said as he looked back on the event. Balang is tall for a Lun Bawang, very earnest and gentle, and a most gifted preacher. His wife, Muring, one of the most attractive and vivacious of Lun Bawang women, very quickly endeared herself to the Kayan people at Long Atip.

In 1952 Amat Lasong, a Lun Bawang from the Lawas church, went to pioneer work amongst the Tagals, and others went to the Baram and Limbang areas. Gradually too, those from other tribes were graduating, some going to Lun Bawang churches for experience, others going to their own people and yet others joining the ranks of the Lun Bawang missionaries to other tribes.

Awang and Gelas were the first Bisaya couple to become missionaries in 1959. They were members of Itai's family and thus the fruit of Ro Bewsher's ministry before the war. They went to the Kenya village of Long Jawe in the rugged mountainous area of the upper reaches of the Rejang river. Gelas, a coastal-dwelling Bisaya, was terrified by the turbulent rapids of the Balui. When Awang went out to the inter-tribal conference, Gelas decided she preferred to endure the isolation of that remote village rather than face the river again.

No pastor was allowed to go to a church until the church had agreed to give at least minimum support and to build a house. No funds came from the Mission for this purpose. At first it was rare for a group to be unwilling to support a pastor, even though the support was, regrettably, only minimal. But as the churches began to lose something of their early enthusiasm, the problem became more pressing, and the end of this period saw increasing difficulties for the pastors.

'It's hard to see the children not getting enough to eat,'

said one pastor from a new area. 'We are sending our two older ones home to their grandparents. It will lighten the burden for my wife and prove less of a strain on the church in the matter of support.'

The Lun Bawang churches had learnt to give and were supporting their own pastors as well as giving to the Lawas Bible school staff, but many of the newer churches were finding it hard. Many hesitated to accept a pastor with a growing family because of the extra support needed. Often this was simply due to the fact that the money was just not available in some of the poorer churches. But the problem was increasing.

Over two hundred pastors and delegates gathered at Lawas for the 1960 inter-tribal conference in December, when the number of churches without pastors was a great concern. Ninety churches had pastors. There were 28 churches asking for pastors, and of these twenty had come into being during 1960. But there were also 76 churches or groups of believers meeting regularly who could not, or in some cases, would not, support pastors.

Added to this was the problem of distance and loneliness for the pastors. One of these new churches asking for a pastor was a group of Iban in Pakan in the Sibu district. This would mean that the SIB and BEM would be stretched over an area five hundred miles long in the interior of a country where rough walking up and down mountains was the only alternative to battling through rapids on the rivers. It was these mountains and rivers which had inspired Stafford Young to conceive the idea of an aircraft programme. His gift of an aircraft had arrived in the very same year that God had led the Mission to the fifteen-year policy. It was not the solution to all these problems, but it certainly made the maximum use of a minimum force.

A woman from the Upper Rejang

CHAPTER 10

RAW EGGS AND AEROPLANES

'IF only I can stay alive until the morning call-up,' was the dominant thought in Ray Cunningham's mind, as he lay helplessly in his little wooden house at Long Geng. Ray had been preaching at Long Jawe, a village two days' upriver from Long Geng, and had been looking for a possible site for an airstrip.

There was an epidemic. Nineteen villagers had already died. Ray had studied the instructions given with his little box of carefully-selected medicines which had so often enabled him to relieve suffering and frequently save life. Every missionary carried one of these little boxes, both for their own use and to meet the incessant calls for medical help in areas where, as yet, there was no medical service. But he had not met anything like this before and his all-too-short course in tropical medicine before he left Australia had not enabled him to diagnose the symptoms of a disease which was, fortunately, somewhat uncommon in those parts.

The Kenyas did their best. Some rubbed egg into his hair, others rice on his back. Yet others, in their eagerness to help, pummelled him according to the ways they had always tried to alleviate sickness. But Ray only got worse.

After four days he realized his only hope was to get to Long Geng where there was a radio and a little pocket-handkerchief airstrip. He himself had built it with the villagers some months before when he and his wife had first moved over from the Upper Baram.

But how could he travel those two days downriver? Ray was the first person ever to take an outboard up into these parts. But he couldn't sit up, let alone drive the boat all day. Tama'Kisun, one of the Kenyas from Long Geng who had gone upriver with him, undertook to try. He'd never driven an outboard before, though of course he was a skilled boatman.

'I remember praying and praying, rolled up in a blanket in the bottom of the dugout canoe,' Ray explained as he looked back.

They got to the mouth of the Linau river all right, but the next morning poor Tama'Kisun just could not make it up the river to Long Geng. He tried and tried, but kept running into the rocks in the rough, turbulent cross currents. They got swamped and lost some of their things. They tried to drag the boat but it was no good.

'Oh Lord, do get us through this,' Ray prayed, and God gave an unexpected answer. He gave Ray the strength to get up and drive the boat himself over the worst part, before he collapsed again. Tama'Kisun then drove the boat to Long Geng.

'I must have been the nearest to dead that I have ever been, when they finally got me to Long Geng,' Ray added. It was no light comment from one who had gained the reputation for being the only man in the Baram who would drive in swollen rivers and seemingly impossible situations. He had had many narrow escapes.

His Kenya friends at Long Geng were loving and helpful but none of them knew what to do any more than Ray did. However, in the middle of the night, one of them gave him a raw egg. He kept it down.

The next morning dawned and Ray knew there would be contact with Lawas on the two-way radio at 6.30 a.m. But his watch had stopped and the call-up sometimes only lasted a few minutes.

'I think it was the raw egg that gave me the strength to turn the knob on the radio,' explained Ray, his pleasant Australian drawl becoming even slower as he lived again those dreadfully uncomfortable hours.

116

The Mission doctor, one of the 'Twelve' who had joined the mission in the early fifties, went down to the hanger for the routine call-up that morning. This had been instituted since the Government had given permission for a transmitter to be installed at Long Tebangan in 1952. In the next few years a network had developed between the various mission bases, making for much greater safety in the aircraft programme, as it was possible to know weather conditions and report delays. It had greatly helped the isolated missionaries too with medical advice, and on this occasion it was a matter of life and death.

The doctor was early. He often went early and would read for a few minutes before switching on, but that morning he started twiddling the knobs straight away. No one was ever early, but there might be something. It was 6.23 a.m. There was a faint voice. He tensed. It was hardly audible, but there it was.

'Testing, testing. Lawas, this is Long Geng.'

Straining every muscle and turning a knob fractionally for better tuning, he could discern Ray's feeble voice.

'Long Geng – Lawas. Long Geng – Lawas, do you read, over?'

'Lawas – Long Geng, request plane as soon as possible, over,' was all Ray could manage.

The contact was made seven minutes ahead of schedule. What a relief swept over Ray as he heard the familiar voice. With hope welling up, he managed to muster a little more strength to describe his symptoms. It didn't take the doctor long to make a diagnosis. 'Typhoid!' he thought, 'and the Mission plane unserviceable!' However, there was a glimmer of hope. Ray had kept down that raw egg, and the chloramphenical in his box was just what he needed.

After making an arrangement for a further call-up, the doctor hurried through the contact with the other stations, where there were fortunately no pressing problems. He crossed the airstrip at the double and disturbed Bruce Morton, the pilot, in the middle of his breakfast.

'What hope of the plane getting into the air today?'

'None, unless there is a miracle,' replied Bruce.

The Shell Oil Company, who had so often been of invaluable assistance in the flying programme, became part of that miracle when they airdropped the spare part that was needed. Bruce and his reliable Lun Bawang assistant Tebari worked throughout the rest of the day.

Tebari Ukab had joined the aircraft team in 1956 and had proved himself not only an adept trainee but a great colleague. He spent the next 20 years keeping the aircraft in service for the use of the church and turned down lucrative jobs and the opportunity to train as a commercial engineer. In an emergency like this, there was no fear that Tebari, any more than Bruce himself, would give up before the job was done. The plane was in the air by the next morning.

The weather was bad and Bruce anxiously looked round at the rapid build-up of clouds as he went in to Long Geng. He had to get through and he did, but could he get out again? Gently the Kenyas carried Ray out to the plane on the aircraft's stretcher. This could replace the passenger seat and it had been used so many times to take the sick out from their distant villages to coastal hospitals. Bruce took off as quickly as he could, but not so quickly as to forget his cockpit drill which always included prayer.

There appeared to be no gap at all in the clouds. Normally he would not have taken off for he had learnt over the hazardous years never to take unnecessary risks. But this was necessary. Ray's life depended on speed.

Round and round they circled, looking this way and that. Nothing. They would have to turn back. It was death for them both to fly into thick cloud in such a mountainous country. Sadly, Bruce began to make his turn. And then he saw it . . . just a small gap, but it was enough. With a quick glance to see that the way still remained open back to Long Geng in case he couldn't get through, he flew towards it, made sure it was clear right through and he was away, headed for the coast and Miri Hospital.

'That raw egg was the best thing you could have had,' was the doctor's comment when Ray was beginning to recover in the comfort of the hospital. Thanks to the aircraft and the marvellous overruling of God he was soon able to return to Long Geng with his wife to continue their work on the translation of the Kenya New Testament.

Long Geng was one of the dozen or so small airstrips which up to that time had been cut out of the jungle in the mountainous interior of Borneo by missionaries of the BEM with the willing help of the villagers concerned. In the decade after 1950, the mission plane actually made 21 first landings on these inland strips. They were all built by hand, using shovels, hoes, spades, bamboo baskets and bark trays for carrying soil, and very occasionally a wheelbarrow. The small payment was usually in tins of sugar, salt and kerosene, flown in instead of being carried over mountains or up rapids. But the reward which they valued most was the possibility of being visited and taught in their new Christian faith.

There had been no strips at all in the interior in 1950, except at Ranau where the Japanese strip had been heavily bombed by the Allied forces. This did not, however, deter Stafford Young who set off the plane programme with his gift of a little two-seater Aeronca aircraft. It had been in use with his brother's flying doctor service in Australia and Stafford had hoped to fly the plane himself until he found that he had to stay at home for family and health reasons. But he had nevertheless given the plane, believing that God would call a pilot.

Bruce Morton, a former officer in the RAAF, had flown over Borneo as a fighter pilot. It was during that time that he had really given his heart to the Lord and God had called him into full-time service. During his two years of training at Melbourne Bible Institute, Borneo had often been in his thoughts but it was not until a few weeks after graduation that God had made the way clear. 'And I will make all my mountains a way and my highways shall be exalted,' was the verse which came to him at that time, but it was only afterwards that he really saw its significance.

Certainly God used Bruce to make the mountains a way for His message. The little Aeronca, named in Melbourne by the Secretary of the Bible Society as *Slamat* (meaning peace or salvation) and then dedicated by Archbishop Mowll in Sydney in July 1949, landed on the new Lawas airstrip in June 1950 after much hold-up.

This strip in itself was one of the indications that God was directing the plane programme. The gift of land for the new Headquarters and Bible School site was reported in the August 1949 *Newsletter* – the very same issue which reported the dedication of the plane in Sydney. Furthermore, when Bruce arrived in Lawas he had found that this new site was 'ideal for the construction of an airstrip', and added that it was 'the only such piece of land known in the area'. At a later date, when the Government began an interior air service, they found a site across the river but this involved vastly more expense and equipment than was appropriate for the Mission.

In 1950 planes landing anywhere other than in the main towns were a novelty and almost the whole population of Lawas and the surrounding villages turned out to welcome and inspect the plane. It was then wheeled into the new hangar and there it stayed for the next six months. The Governments of Sabah and Sarawak were pondering the question of how they could undertake the responsibility of allowing a very small single-engined aircraft without radio to fly in the interior where no other aircraft flew.

Permission was finally given in December 1950, and Bruce began the process of opening up the interior to flying. Until 1954 he was totally alone. If he crashed, there was no other plane that could come to help.

For the first few months he could only use the few coastal airfields, part of the Ranau strip which was not damaged, and the new Lawas strip. When the tide was out he could also land on the sandbank at Sipitang, just ten minutes flying time from Lawas over the border in Sabah. But even these few strips began to cut travelling time radically. The greatest saving, however, would come when interior strips were built.

On 8th June 1951, just under a year since *Slamat* had landed at Lawas, Bruce set off to make his first landing on the first of these interior strips. As he flew towards Long Atip, with no radio contact with the ground, he wondered whether the strip would be ready and how difficult the landing would be.

'Even as I flew, I saw something that I had never seen before,' he wrote at the time. 'With the rising sun behind the plane, a perfect, complete rainbow encircled the *Slamat*. An inspiring sight.' God's promises were real and he flew on.

Arriving at the strip, he saw the smoky fire which was the prearranged signal that it was all right to land. After flying low over the area to inspect the strip, he brought the plane in to a safe landing. A crowd, led by the Penghulu, quickly and excitedly gathered round the plane. They had never seen a plane close up before, and to have one land on a little strip running parallel to their longhouse was almost unbelievable.

Six months later, Bruce was making a first landing at Meligan in Tagal country, tucked behind the 7,000 foot Crocker Range, and then at the Lun Bawang village of Long Semadoh in the Upper Trusan. At the latter he found the strip was only six yards wide. No damage was sustained but a little more work had to be done before he could take off again.

These were the first three, after which year by year more strips were added until there was a whole network from Ranau in the north, through Meligan and Long Pa Sia to the south of Sabah, then over into Sarawak, Ba Kelalan in the far interior of Lun Bawang country, to Pa Mein in the Kelabit Highlands, then on to the Baram and into the Third (now known as the Seventh) Division.

As the first to land aircraft in the interior of Borneo, Bruce had opened the way for others, so that by the end of the first decade the Government was beginning to consider an air service. Now there is a radio and airways network throughout the interior.

An exceptionally good pilot was essential for such pioneering, but without the protecting hand of God such a programme could never have been achieved without serious accident. Perhaps this is best illustrated by an incident in the early days which caused much agonized prayer at Lawas because of lack of radio contact. On short strips, none more than 450 yards and some considerably less, it was essential to be able to touch down in exactly the right place and this Bruce could do – except once.

On 16th October 1953 he took off for Long Pa Sia. He had landed there before but this was to be the first landing after some improvements had been made to the drainage.

Landing as usual from the hill-bound end to the west, he aimed to touch down near the end of the strip. The aircraft inexplicably 'floated', although speed and position were correct, so that it didn't actually land until halfway down the strip. Several severe jolts brought the aircraft to a stop and caused the engine to cut as the tail wheel dug into the mud and pulled out.

Relieved and somewhat shaken, Bruce climbed out of the aircraft, and started to walk back along the strip. The grass was rather long as the village people had tired of waiting for the plane. He found that there was water on the strip for a hundred yards but this could not be seen from the air due to the long grass. Had his wheels touched, he would almost certainly have flipped over. Even if he had not been hurt, it would have been an impossible job to get the plane out of such a remote place.

'Underneath [literally on this occasion!] are the everlasting arms.'

As there was no radio at Long Pa Sia, Bruce had told his wife Ruth and those at Lawas not to expect him until the next day, but the dawning of that day showed the strip softer through night rain. It was the same the next day. The villagers worked on making a bamboo mat to cover the worst part but as Bruce walked down the strip on the 20th he found there was still not enough. He thought of Ruth and the strain for her every time he took off, not knowing what was happening. He felt helpless but then he suddenly noticed an unexpected strong wind coming directly down the strip from the west. He pondered the possibility of a take-off from the east end. He had never attempted that way before because of the grade of the strip. Also a take-off from the east involved negotiating the mountains near to the west end after take-off. But the strong wind would help with lift, and already 40 yards of strip beyond the centre were safe with the bamboo mat. He decided to try.

'I let off the brakes and the plane rolled forward on the sodden ground,' he wrote. 'The bamboo mat seemed to come quickly near but just before reaching it the plane lifted into the buoyant air.'

He reached Lawas three days late. But for the wind it would have been a lot later.

The one occasion when there was a major accident was three years later in somewhat similar circumstances to those at Long Pa Sia, but a very different situation. It was the only major accident to any of the Mission planes in the whole of the 28 years of flying up to the present day.

Bad weather closed in unusually quickly, and Bruce was forced to land at Long Atip in blinding rain on Monday

30th April 1956. The strip was partially flooded and the inevitable happened. The plane's wheels hit the water and it flipped over, but neither Bruce nor his passengers were hurt. Long Atip was the only airstrip in the interior from which the plane could be disassembled and taken downriver. Several months later Bruce was able to write,

'As we move further away in time from the experience . . . the conviction emerges that this was allowed of God. Added to the many experiences of God's undertaking at the time of the accident itself, more causes for praise have become apparent, not least the discovery of very serious corrosion in four of the main members of the fuselage. If this had continued unnoticed and the plane continued to fly, it could have caused a much more serious accident.' The defect occurred under clips fitted by the makers which are not examined in the normal course of maintenance.

That accident happened to the second BEM aircraft, an Auster Aiglet, given by an Australian man in the transport business. The reliable little Aeronca had proved too small.

'You don't use a five-ton truck to take a ten-ton load,' was Charlie Davis's comment when he had given the Aiglet, and with a businessman's foresight he had given a spare engine as well. That was in 1951, when Stafford Young had been in England, mainly with a view to forming a Home Council for the BEM and doing some deputation work to make the BEM known. But he had been in the right spot to purchase the new aircraft when it was needed.

Just the week before the Long Atip accident, the Shell Oil Company had given an Auster Autocar to the Mission. Its use had been rendered nearly superfluous for them by the introduction of helicopters, and it needed a new engine. Knowing the Mission had a spare engine, they made the generous gift of the aircraft, together with about a thousand pounds' worth of spare parts.

About 150 guests were present on 24th April 1956 at Shell Aerodrome at Anduke, Seria, when the presentation was made to the Mission. Mr R. E. Hales, managing director of BMP and SOL, gave an address on that occasion which was reported in the April 28th issue of the newspaper *Salam*. Mr Hales had made some general remarks about missionary work and then added:

'Without wishing to single out the work of any one Mission in particular, the purpose for which we have gathered today does, I think, justify mention of the quite romantic development of the BEM and its unique achievements in the field of communications . . .' And then he further added, 'to anyone acquainted with the topography of the interior and the hazards of its mist-enshrouded mountains and valleys, the Mission's aviation achievements using small single-engined aircraft without benefit of radio aids – were nothing short of miraculous.'

Within a week of the accident to the Aiglet, the Autocar was in the air and it had the added advantage of being able to take HF radio without drastically reducing the payload.

God had answered many prayers to make the whole aircraft programme possible, but contrary to the belief of some sceptics, the Mission planes never relied on prayer at the expense of efficient maintenance and care. To begin with the Quantas engineer in Labuan did whatever needed to be done but Bruce was soon able to do much of his own work. By 1955 Ken Cooper had completed his engineering exams and this meant that for the first time the annual inspection for the certificate of airworthiness could be carried out at Lawas, saving a lot of valuable time and money. Under Ken's tuition, Bruce who had already built up considerable experience in maintenance, was able to take his engineering exams. In addition, under Bruce's tuition, Ken was also soon able to add to his commercial pilot's licence sufficient experience in Bornean conditions to qualify as the Mission's second pilot. Tebari Ukab has been mentioned as joining the team in 1956, but still there was need for another pilot-engineer.

Harold Parsons was 40 when God called him into missionary work. He was running a successful little business and was puzzled by what seemed to be God's leading.

'I can't be a missionary', he thought, thinking an ability to preach or translate, or medical training were the things that were needed. 'But maybe there is something practical I could do.'

He sold his business and used the money to train as a pilot-engineer, getting jobs crop-dusting in order to build up his flying hours. He left for Borneo on 21st July 1957, fully qualified, and with experience with Auster Aircraft. Initially he went out for twelve months to relieve Ken Cooper who had to go to Australia for further training and leave, but at the end of that time he was asked to stay on and complete the normal four years' tour. Bruce then began to orientate him to interior flying, and he and his wife Hazel soon became fully-fledged members of the missionary team.

Before the end of the first decade of flying, the Aiglet had been repaired and sold and a Piper Tripacer had been given to the Mission. This time it was a businessman in England whom God used. A little old lady had given him a copy of the *BEM Newsletter* when he first became a Christian. He was a member of Westminster Chapel. Dr Martyn Lloyd-Jones, the minister there, together with John Stott, had accepted Stafford Young's invitation in 1951 to become the Advisory Council to the little BEM council which he had set up in England. Westminster was also the home church of the first honorary secretary in England, Eric Pearson, who worked relentlessly and alone for six years until in 1957 he was joined by John Smith, a businessman who had come to know the Lord some years before while serving with the Army in Malaya. Three of the English missionaries who had joined the Australian and New Zealand members of the BEM team also came from Westminster Chapel. It was fitting, therefore, that this new plane should be called *Westminster Chapel* and given at a time when the opening up of new areas demanded its higher performance. Communication lines had been greatly extended and the plane programme was becoming ever more necessary to make the maximum use of a minimum force. It was not long before this same businessman had given a second Tripacer, this time called *Sidang Injil Borneo* after the growing Church which he saw emerging. These two planes continued to give vital service over the years, until they too had to be replaced in 1970 by a Helio Courier.

The first plane began its active service, as we have seen, the very year that God led the Mission to the fifteen-year policy. Successive gifts of planes and pilots, including help from the Missionary Aviation Fellowship, have been the means of saving time, energy and the expense of days and weeks of travel. A typical 10-day journey was cut to 45 minutes and the cost of running the aircraft was half the cost of the guide and carriers needed. In this way vital energy could be put more effectively into the urgent teaching of the church, together with the equally urgent need to translate the Word of God which was being taught.

A Dusun woman

CHAPTER 11

WRITTEN INSTRUCTIONS

A DEACON who had given up considerable prosperity to serve the church became pastor to a village not far from the beautiful, hilly government outstation of Keningau in the central highlands of Sabah. His wife fell sick and she was carried to the Government hospital where she quickly recovered. Too quickly, perhaps, as she was attractive and one of the medical orderlies found her irresistible.

Sadly the pastor took her back to their home village, as he could no longer continue as a pastor. But she did not admit her guilt. Several of her friends went to her to talk with her but she would not listen, and then they called a missionary from Lawas but he met with the same response.

Finally Balang Selutan, who by this time had returned from Kayan to Lun Bawang country, went to talk to her.

'How did you get on?' the missionary asked.

'Oh, all right. She repented,' was Balang's somewhat matter-of-fact reply.

'Balang, how is it that the rest of us tried and got nowhere?' the puzzled missionary queried.

'I just read to her verses of Scripture that deal with adultery.'

'But what did you say?'

'Oh, nothing. I just sat and waited for the Holy Spirit to speak to her.'

In fact, with typical patience, Balang had waited for half an hour and the Holy Spirit had used the words of Scripture to convict her and bring her to real repentance.

Incidents such as this serve to re-emphasize the truth stated by William Tyndale four hundred years ago. 'I perceived by experience,' he wrote, 'how that it was impossible to stablysh the laye people in any truth except the Scripture were playnly layde before their eyes in their mother tongue.' The BEM team had always been aware of this but was not always in a position to do very much about it.

In the pre-war period, the demands of constant travelling and teaching had made it very difficult to give the priority to translation that the missionaries would have liked. Post-war, too, so many calls were coming from all directions and travelling was so time-consuming that it was difficult to see how anyone was going to be able to give enough time to translate one New Testament, let alone several.

Then, as we have seen, the plane was beginning to deal with the time factor and the fifteen-year policy gave a new sense of urgency not only to the teaching programme but also to translation.

'Schools may be established and a people educated in another language, but without the Word of God in its own mother tongue, a church will not stand alone and grow in grace. For the church does not consist of buildings, organizations or educated men and women. The church consists of ordinary people; of old ladies sitting back in the village minding the grandchildren, of the old men governing the village, of men and women going out daily to their rice farms; of children growing up to be ordinary people. The earlier these ordinary people have the Scriptures in their own language, the earlier the church will develop under the instruction of the Holy Spirit and become independent of the missionaries from another land.'[1]

Translation work became of paramount importance, but this could not be done until the various unwritten languages had been reduced to writing. The 1952

[1] *From Every Tribe*, page 15.

conference therefore decided that there should be a drive to get orthographies finalized and standardized in all the languages in which the Mission was actually working at the time. This work could be speeded up thanks to the training which some of the missionaries had by now received from the Summer Institute of Linguistics.

An article in the April 1953 Newsletter gives some idea of how linguistic training was combined with urgent prayer to deal with some rather tricky problems in Dusun, one of the more difficult of the languages.

'On arrival we found God had gone before and provided a good range of excellent language helpers. In two weeks God had given us a phonemic alphabet. This of course means the smallest number of letters to cover all the significant sounds and thus eliminate spelling difficulties. When this was tried out it worked. Dusun adults and young people who had some previous knowledge of reading Malay could read and spell Dusun quite easily with the alphabet in a very short time.'

But the alphabet problems were not the main difficulty which had been facing the Gollans and others working on Dusun. There was the complicated grammar, or rather the lack of any systematized knowledge of it. The verb was incredibly complex, and not infrequently the very eager and helpful Dusuns would say about two different forms,

'They are different . . . they are very similar . . . oh, they are the same.'

'Then, as in any language there was the host of little words which can only be defined as in the *Oxford English Dictionary* with a series of examples of their usage. As one of the Dusun language helpers said:

'"You must use them but I cannot tell you what they mean in Malay. Malay doesn't seem to need them but we cannot talk without them."'

Of course Malay did have some, but they were different and used in different places. There was no alternative to the painstaking collection of hundreds of examples of these elusive but vital little words without which Dusun is not real Dusun, Malay is not real Malay and English is not real English. They vitally affected the verb form but even after many weeks, they still remained a mystery. Here was a particular opportunity to see God's hand at work. The article continues,

'Thanking God for taking us out of our depth, we and our prayer partners asked Him for a sufficient unfolding of the grammar in the two and a half months available. God gave us the first clue on 3rd November when the Scripture Gift Mission were remembering us on their day of prayer. He gave us answers to (another problem) on 4th December, that is the day after the BEM day of prayer.' He continued to unfold the fascinating grammatical structure of Dusun so that the Gollans were able to take up the task of translation of the New Testament in consultation with those working in other areas of the Dusun language.

The Gollans had various helpers with the translation but the bulk of the New Testament was translated by Dayeh Bantasan. When a boy of 14, Dayeh had had a serious wound on his knee. Unable to walk, he was left behind alone in the house when the family went to the farm each day. Of course there was no medical help available for someone who could not do the five-day walk to the coast in those days. He had time to think and dream. One day he dreamt of help which would come and a few weeks later Trevor White and Kentuni arrived at his village.

Due to lack of medical help, Dayeh was now permanently lame, but he had heard a little of the good news and he wanted more. He hobbled the eight miles to Ranau, followed by his wrinkled old mother. There they stayed in order to learn about the Christian way and for Dayeh to give what help he could to the missionaries as they tried to learn his language.

A few years later God called Dayeh to help with the New

Testament. Although lame, Dayeh was strong and active and he found the work tedious at first but his sense of call kept him for seven years, in spite of ups and downs of health. Finally, when the New Testament was nearing completion, Dayeh became too weak to carry on and in August 1969 he went to be with his Lord whom he had served for twenty years.

Finding language helpers proved a fascinating problem for the Kayan New Testament. Different helpers were tried and samples of their work given to people in different areas. One was from an old man with a marvellous command of his own language.

'Oh, yes, that is wonderful Kayan language,' was the reaction. 'It is very deep. It is so deep that we can't understand it.'

Then there was some translation by some of the boys in school.

'Yes, it is good. We love the stories. But what a pity it is in children's language.'

The missionary went on to a new area and found a young man of noble class, a young prince who knew it too! He loved ordering people around. They translated Mark's Gospel.

'Yes, it is good,' the people said, 'It is the Lord's word. But it sounds as if it has been translated by someone who is proud.'

Then the missionary started to work with Taman Ngau who was a man in his late twenties, quiet, sober-thinking, respected by his people. He was a deacon who truly loved the Lord. They did some translation together. It was just right. Taman Ngau continued to work until the New Testament was completed in 1968.

Good language helpers are like gold and obviously vital to the task of translation. The Tagal New Testament, which was not begun until towards the end of the fifties, had the valuable help of a headman's son. He was passionately concerned with the use of his own language. When he turned to politics, it seemed impossible to find anyone as good, but the Lord called his brother-in-law. Sumayong, a young man, was the son of a former paramount chief in the area who had been of such standing that when he died he had been replaced by three men. Sumayong, though perhaps lacking some of the drive and enthusiasm of his brother-in-law, was very gifted and had had the privilege of a full primary education. His father had sent him to a Chinese school initially when there were no other schools. When Malay education came to his area, Sumayong learnt a third language to continue his schooling. He had a keen mind and saw the draft New Testament through to completion, in spite of many temptations to give up.

Tubu Padan, translator of the Lun Bawang New Testament, had also been tempted to give up. In fact on one occasion he had actually gone home but he was persuaded by the deacons in his village to return and finish the job. As he looked back from his position of Chairman of the SIB in Sarawak during 1977, nearly twenty years later, he was glad that he had seen the job through, in spite of the hardships.

'Now I look back,' he said, 'I'm glad I wasn't paid. The Lun Bawang have changed so much through the Word of God and I am very happy that God called me to translate it.'

Madge Belcher had actually started the Lun Bawang New Testament with Racha at the village where he was a pastor. They translated Matthew's Gospel before Racha's many responsibilities forced him to hand over to Tubu.

Translation is hard, tedious work and Madge kept a diary of their day-to-day progress. One day reads,

'Racha and I impatient with each other over translation. Both felt miserable. I apologized and we both prayed.'

Another day: 'Work is hard. Both practically fainting by lunch time.'

But then there is a note to say how wonderfully Madge was finding the Word of God feeding her own soul and she adds, 'This has been a very happy time.'

Racha too was finding that the word which he was translating was speaking to him. They came to Matthew 18.

'Does this really mean we should go and speak to those who are sinning?'

When Madge answered that that was what it said, Racha replied,

'Then why have you missionaries not taught us to do this?'

Madge apologized. A few weeks later when she was at Lawas, Racha wrote to her explaining how he had put Matthew 18.15–17 into practice.

'I am very happy because the Lord has been helping me in my care of the church here . . . when I went to exhort the Penghulu, he straightaway confessed his sin, so did his son. Many others did likewise.'

The word of God in his own language had challenged Racha. Very humbly and prayerfully and waiting for the opportunities which God gave him, he went from one to another to plead with them to get right with the Lord. It was not long before there was a new consciousness of sin in the whole village and a desire for cleansing. The Spirit of God came down upon them to meet that need. It had all begun because one godly man read a portion of the word of God in his own language.

Translating an ordinary book is no easy task. But there is an added difficulty in translating the Bible. There is the responsibility to translate so accurately, as well as readably, that a whole church will be established and not led astray.

For a year the word used for 'Spirit' in Tagal was *Karuruo*. *Karuruo* was certainly 'spirit'. It meant the spirit which left a man at death to go on into the next life.

'Is God dead?' asked a deacon who had been a pillar of the church for many years.

'Dead? Oh no, of course He is not dead. He's alive,' replied the horrified missionary.

'But He must be dead. How else could He have a *Karuruo*?' Translation work was set aside for a time while the missionary gave yet further teaching on the living God and the Resurrection. Then a long discussion ensued and the word was changed in the draft translation. Fortunately it had not yet been printed, but how easy it would have been for this word to remain to confuse the Church – indeed to lead them astray from the idea of the ever-living God who raised Jesus Christ from the dead.

But the right word may take many years to find, even if it is a less vital word than 'spirit'.

The Kayan translator had been five years in Kayan country and she still had not found the way the Kayans expressed the idea of 'whether' – 'I don't know whether he will come (or not)'. She relates the story of the sort of incident that is so important to a translator. How easily the opportunity could have been missed!

'Here comes that old lady again! She talks . . . and I always have to tell her I'm very busy and will have to get to work now, or say "Oh, you're going now! I'll walk up the longhouse with you". But today I ask the Lord for the patience to sit with her until she is ready to go, even if that is not until evening. She prattles on and on and on . . . . What was that? I beg your pardon, say that again! There it was. "I don't know whether he'll come or whether he won't come." Thank you Lord, I'll put that in my dictionary.'

The rewards for all the painstaking research are a hundredfold when the New Testament becomes meaningful to the church. A few verses of Romans chapter 1 had been translated into Kayan for teaching purposes and were being read to a group of folk sitting on the longhouse floor.

'Is that really what God said?'

'When was it written?'

'How did they know about us Kayans that long ago?'

Years later the whole of Romans had been completed. The translators had battled their way through problems such as 'reconciliation'. The Kayan word implied 'to give a gift of gongs and knives sprinkled with the blood of a sacrificial chicken'. The word 'sacrifice' to a Kayan could mean 'to whisper a message in the ear of a pig, kill it, then take out the liver and read the spots to receive the answer from the spirits'.

They had struggled through a great but difficult book and the missionary commented to Taman Ngau:

'Romans is a very difficult book. I don't understand it fully.'

'Why,' replied Taman Ngau; 'read it in Kayan. It's easy in Kayan.'

Each one of the languages presented different problems but the Church must have the Word of God. In the early fifties, the Bible Societies were feeling that perhaps time and money ought to be given more to the large language areas, and tribes of a few thousands would take a fairly low priority. But one Bible Society Secretary visited the inter-tribal convention at Pa Mein in 1955.

'These people must have the New Testament,' was his comment, and from then on he kept urging the Belchers to 'get on and finish the New Testament'.

The National Bible Society of Scotland, helped by the New Zealand Bible Society, generously undertook to finance the Lun Bawang New Testament. The indebtedness of the church to the Bible Societies was further increased by their agreeing to two special features. They included a cross reference system and wide margins so that these New

Testaments could be study books, thus compensating a little for lack of Bible Study aids. They also provided hard-wearing, insect-proofed covers as the books were carried everywhere through the jungle into longhouses and farm huts.

Another NBSS Secretary visited the field in 1958 and he too went home to stress the need, not just for the Lun Bawang, but for all the languages. He wrote at the time,

'I have seen how important and how urgent is the need for Scriptures in the languages of the tribespeople. I have learned how the Christians begin more rapidly to grow in grace and how the church advances just as soon as ever some portion of Scripture is available in their tongues, even in its initial typed or mimeographed form . . . many of the people are eager to learn to read and they appear to have a highly-developed sense of the authority of Scripture. They seem to be a people who not only read or hear the Word of God, but who also want to do it.'

High priority was given to translating New Testaments during the fifties and sixties, but of course time was also given to hymn books. These were particularly useful amongst semi-literate tribespeople as they could be taught to those who could not yet read. Then time also had to be given to the preparing of reading primers and the teaching of hundreds of people throughout the interior to read.

Lun Bawang was the first New Testament to reach the printing stage. Begun in 1952, the actual translation was completed by 1956 but then followed several years of arduous checking – checking for routine matters such as spelling, punctuation, consistency, then more vital checking for accuracy and harmony between the Gospels, which involved about 2,000 Scripture phrases and words to be compared. Further, there was a most vital check for language with Lun Bawang from Indonesia, as they would also be using the New Testament. It was not until 1962 that advance copies reached Lawas.

6th May 1962 was a special Bible Sunday at Lawas. A packed church watched the representatives of the Bible Societies of Scotland and New Zealand present to the SIB a copy of the Lun Bawang New Testament. It was gilt-edged and bound in deep red leather.

The Lun Bawang was the first New Testament but it was followed by others during the next few years. In early 1969 the first printed Tagal Scriptures arrived. The draft for the whole New Testament had been completed in 1966 but as the missionaries had gone on extended leave that year, it had been impossible to check all of it. The Bible Societies, quite contrary to their normal policy of only publishing whole New Testaments with hard backs, generously printed a good half of the New Testament in Tagal in an attractive cover similar to the Lun Bawang New Testament. By 1970, the Kayan New Testament proofs were being read. The Dusun New Testament manuscript had been sent off to the Bible Societies for printing, as had 40 per cent of the Kenya New Testament. In Penan, half the New Testament had been translated and the book of Acts was printed. An anthology of Old and New Testaments had been printed in Kayan, Dusun and Kenya and the first Old Testament was well on the way in Lun Bawang.

Madge Belcher had given some time between finishing the New and starting the Old Testament in Lun Bawang, to Kelabit Scriptures, a translation of which had been begun by Kuda Pengiran. Kuda was a Kelabit who had entered Bible School in 1949, and he had made a rough draft of several books in his own language. But when the Kelabits saw the attractive, hard-wearing whole New Testaments in Lun Bawang, they decided that their languages were sufficiently closely related for them to be able to use the printed books.

Sometimes, after printing, there was difficulty at first in encouraging the tribal folk to read in their own language.

But an incident from Tagal country can speak for the whole field.

Ansaning, a deacon, owned a Malay New Testament and was fond of reading it. There was a trace of pride in the man because he could read Malay. Matthew's Gospel in his own language had arrived in his village. He did not bother to buy a copy. But he was keen to learn and travelled some distance to a short-term Bible school which was being held. All the studies at that particular school were taken from the new Tagal translation of Matthew and so he reluctantly bought a copy and began to read it.

He soon found himself reading it all the time in and out of school. After a month he went home, excited about God's word in his own language and reading it with fair fluency. Almost against his own will, Ansaning demonstrated the old truth that Scriptures in the mother tongue penetrate to the heart and mean far more to the people than in even a familiar trade language.

Language, as Edwin Smith puts it in the title of his book, is 'the shrine of a people's soul.'

CHAPTER 12

SPONTANEOUS EXPANSION

Ansaning owed his new Christian life to the willingness of a former headhunting enemy to go to his village in Sabah. Amat Lasong's father had made daring raids on the Tagals for heads in his younger days.

'I wouldn't dare go the Tagals unless God had called me,' was Amat's comment to the District Officer when he set off to pioneer a work among them in 1952. He knew headhunting had been stopped by law, but he also knew that the Tagals were very skilled with jungle poisons.

Amat was one of the first Lawas Lun Bawang to become a Christian. He had had a spiritual hunger when quite a young lad so that when he began to hear the rumours which were affecting the whole Lun Bawang tribe in the thirties, he became very interested. One day, someone said that this Tuhan Yesus (Lord Jesus) had arrived in the Trusan and he set off to investigate. In fact it was the Davidsons! The message that Amat heard from them satisfied him. He became as much of a Christian as he knew how, and for the next months made frequent visits to learn more.

He was better off than many of the Lun Bawang as his spiritual hunger had kept him from the worst of his tribe's debauchery and he was building himself a house for which he had prepared boards. But when the sickly Lun Bawang in the Trusan were having difficulty completing the building of their church, he provided fifty of those precious hand-hewn boards to finish the building. Some time later Amat and the Lawas Lun Bawang built their own church but the Japanese burnt it down. It was the charred remains of this church and its replacement which greeted Hudson Southwell on his return to Borneo.

Although over forty, Amat went into Bible school. Learning was difficult but he persisted and could struggle through his Malay New Testament which he did at every conceivable moment. While in school, he began to be aware that there was an urgent need to go to the Tagals. There was no missionary to answer the persistent calls for teaching and so he 'graduated' from school, only just literate. He became the first Lun Bawang to pioneer, without missionary help at first, the establishment of a church in a former enemy tribe.

The BEM had had intermittent contact with the Tagals since first travelling through the fringes of their territory in 1937 and the burden they felt for them is frequently mentioned in the reports. The Tagals were regarded as 'treacherous, unstable and degraded' by those who had had to put down numerous uprisings. Missionaries from Indonesia had tried to preach to them in 1930, but had had to leave due to the unpredictable reactions among them. And their degradation was plain for all to see. A visitor in 1948 wrote, 'It would be impossible to describe the filth, squalor, the disease and degradation found in these longhouses', but he added the cheerful note that it was coupled with a great desire for teaching.

Degraded they might be due to their excessive alcoholism and the taboos and omens which seriously affected their health – no pregnant or nursing mother was allowed to eat vegetables, their main source of iron. But they were not without great skill and craftsmanship. Many a craftsman made his own blowpipe, shaping the wood with a slight curve, so that gravity would straighten it out when in the firing position. And they were famous for their unique sprung dance floors, long before the trampoline became popular in the west.

Nevertheless, they were dying out. The 1950 census

figures showed the population to be 18,724, a decrease of about 5,000 since 1930, and the Government began to press the Mission to go to them, saying, 'the situation was so critical amongst these people that their only hope was the commencement of missionary work amongst them'. Was this attitude perhaps another result of the change seen in the Lun Bawang?

The Belchers went with some Bible school students to the big Easter *tamu* (trade gathering) in 1950 in Sipitang, just over the Sabah border from Lawas. They had a meeting with some fifty Tagals who had come to the *tamu* from the interior and had seen the change in the Lun Bawang over recent years. They pleaded for a teacher to go to them but there was no one available. The Belchers could see no alternative but to risk an experiment. They suggested that the Tagals choose two young married couples to go into the Bible school.

When Racha and Amat visited Meligan, the village from which the Tagals came, they found five couples ready to go to school. But due to their taboos and omens, the rice crop had failed. The village was near starvation and would not be able to support any of them. Friends in Australia, through what was known as the 'Birthday Band', agreed to support two couples and so Impau, younger brother of the Penghulu, and Lutus, with their wives, went into Bible School.

One of the teachers in the Bible school wrote to these friends in Australia, describing the Tagals as 'raw heathen, no idea of living settled, ordered lives, always seeking self-interest first. As sure as I saw Lutus approaching, I would know he was after rice or kerosene or salt. . . .'

Nevertheless, when vacation time came, Impau and Lutus gathered all the Meligan people together and shared what they had been learning in school. The village became so keen that they offered to build a house and an airstrip if only some missionaries would go to them.

Meanwhile, the Belchers, while holidaying in Labuan in January 1951, were invited to meet Sir Ralph Hone, Governor of Sabah, and Mr Combe, resident for Labuan and the Interior. They found 'both these men were very desirous for the Mission to commence work amongst the Tagals and promised to give every assistance in beginning such a work'.

Opportunity came for Alan Belcher to visit Meligan in August 1951. Together with Impau and Lutus, he took a number of meetings over the next few days and also looked for a site for an airstrip. He measured it out, 400 yards by 15 yards wide. Fortunately there were no trees but even so, before Alan went on further to visit the Lun Bawang church at Pa Matang, he changed the width to 12 yards. Eleven days later he returned to find things well under way. But they might well not have been.

The Penghulu had decided the project was too big and was going to call it off – the width had been changed just in time. Further, the only tools they had were six or eight large hoes, their jungle knives and little axes. The earth could only be moved by carrying it in hands or crude sledges made of pieces of bark.

Added to that were the taboos connected with pregnancy. At such a time neither man nor wife was allowed to dig because it was symbolic of digging a grave. The wife or baby would die. But Impau and Lutus not only supervised the airstrip, they taught the people what they had been learning about freedom from bondage through Christ. Soon it was noticed that one after another who had previously only been willing to cut grass, joined in the earth work. It was a great step of faith to break with age-old customs, and the airstrip was finished in time for Bruce Morton's first landing. A few months later Impau and Lutus and their wives asked for baptism, and this was when Amat went to begin his ministry at Meligan.

Amat taught ceaselessly. 45 men met in 'school' every

morning and worked their farms in the afternoons. There was a daily pre-dawn prayer meeting for everyone. In the evenings, he ran special classes for those he had selected as church leaders. On Saturday nights there was a steady stream of visitors, at first to the pastor's house and then to temporary little huts which sprang up all round. They lived too far away to be able to get to the Sunday service on Sunday, so they came the night before. Soon they were building slightly more permanent houses and a football field, and a small community was growing up.

Amat had arrived in November 1952 and by the following February it was reported that ten couples had been baptised, two deacons had been appointed and already a number of men had accompanied Amat on preaching trips. Amat assumed that young Christians would want to pass on what they knew. In addition to his own travelling he also sent them off on their own, having taught them carefully first and translated a few hymns for them to memorize and sing. Even when they went off to visit relatives or on trading trips, he would always assume they had shared their faith and sung these hymns which contained the essential truths.

'What was the response when you told them about the Lord?' was usually his first question on their return. Hearing this question at a later date, a missionary noted to his shame that he would probably have asked, 'Did you have an opportunity to speak about the Lord?' – a question which reflected so much less confidence in the working of the Spirit in these young Christians.

While Amat carried on his establishment of the church at Meligan and supervised the ever-increasing expansion outwards from there, missionaries, Bible school students and pastors, visited further afield.

One of these parties included Impau and Sabilar his wife, and Pastor Upai Baru, recently returned from the Upper Baram. They walked for six weeks up and down mountains to Pensiangan and then up the 114 miles of bridle track to Keningau. Several of these visits were made over the next few years, the missionary usually wearing out two pairs of sandshoes during the six weeks of walking involved.

In the Tagul river area, towards Pensiangan, the missionary was fascinated to see a little round disc of wood with seven holes in it and a small wooden peg in one of them. What pagan significance did this have?

'We have heard that Christians keep one day in seven differently. We move the peg round each day and when we come to the seventh, we don't work.'

People ten days' walk from Meligan had heard what had been happening there and were eager to hear more.

A missionary couple was now available to go to live amongst the Tagals but it was at this point that a serious problem arose. The Government were pressing hard for the Mission to establish a work in an area which wanted education rather than Christian teaching before they would allow them to go elsewhere. The Mission found themselves in a similar position to that in the Limbang before the war. They faced the prospect of battling in an unresponsive area for years while the spiritually hungry starved.

A photograph in the *Weekly Times* changed the situation. Paying a courtesy call to the Resident's office, the missionary found himself invited to visit the Resident at his home that evening. As he went in, the masterful photograph on the wall caught his eye.

'Haven't I seen that photograph in the *Weekly Times*?' he asked.

'Yes, it was published.'

'It's magnificent, and well worthy of publication.'

A lengthy and warm-hearted discussion followed on a subject dear to the hearts of both.

A trivial incident, one might say. But God used it to

warm the heart of the Resident and to give an opportunity to explain the reasons why the Mission wanted to send a couple to Meligan rather than the area he wanted to see occupied. He gave his permission.

On arrival, the missionaries found that the people were still very bound by their pagan dietary customs although they had been Christians for two years. One of the missionaries, who was a doctor, was looking at a long queue of very sickly patients one day, when two women came puffing up the notched log into his house. In their arms they each carried a sickly, emaciated baby. Mothers and babies were all desperately anaemic. A few iron tablets could have cured the women, even though the babies looked beyond hope. But the doctor did not want to force them into endless debts with the Chinese traders at the coast, from whom they would have to obtain iron pills when the missionary was not there.

Calling the Penghulu, he suggested that he should arrange for these two women to be supervised in the eating of vegetables three times a day.

'We'll die,' they complained, remembering all too clearly their pagan taboos. But they were Christians now and so were eventually persuaded to try.

At the end of four weeks, these women could climb the notched log without panting and even one of the babies was considerably better. Within a year, the health of the whole area had been affected. The news spread. Soon even the pagans round about had broken with that particular taboo and were planting and eating vegetables, and some were wanting Christian teaching. Even the side effects of the Gospel were acting as bridges into other areas.

By this time Impau had graduated and the Penghulu insisted that his young brother should return to Meligan. Amat moved on to Ulu Tomani, two more hard days' walking from Meligan, over the mountains to the east. They had heard from the Meligan folk and were asking for a pastor, being willing to support him and having already built a house. Fifty families turned en masse to Christianity but both here and at Meligan the counter-attack was not long in coming. After the initial enthusiasm and a momentous step of faith in turning away from the fear of spirits, there rapidly grew up a problem of nominalism. Regular attendance at church, turning away from drunkenness and adultery, and even going out telling others what they knew, all became substitutes for a true faith, and the urgent need was to get in and teach.

In 1958 the missionary went to ask for permission to enter the area from Ulu Tomani down the Padas Valley to Tenom after incessant calls for three years. The District Officer was surprised and sceptical about the request, feeling that the Mission was behaving somewhat shadily.

'In fact you have already occupied the area,' he said with a certain amount of annoyance.

The Mission had studiously avoided preaching in the whole area, knowing that the Government was still very sensitive about its zoning policy. But Ulu Tomani Tagals passed through the valley for trade, and Meligan Tagals had been to the Padas to get work.

'We cannot stop the Tagals talking,' the missionary pointed out. The DO reluctantly accepted that it was 'spontaneous expansion' and he could do nothing to stop it. Permission was given for the BEM to enter the area officially.

Immediately, at every turn, there were requests for a pastor. Village after village, having built a pastor's house and sometimes a little church as well, was calling for someone to go and teach. Perhaps the most interesting request came from a group of between a hundred and two hundred at the mouth of the Tomani river. A church had sprung up as a result of the preaching of a renegade Lun Bawang deacon.

Ten years previously this man had been a deacon in an Upper Trusan church. He had fallen into sin and had been disciplined by his church. Ashamed but unwilling to repent, he had taken a Government job in Tagal country. After eight years God had met him.

The calls for pastors were not restricted to the Padas area, however. It was not long before a request came from the Keningau district, three hours' jeep ride from Tenom. A new Christian from the Padas had visited his relatives there and they wanted to become Christians. Four days inland from there, yet others had heard the Gospel from a Lun Bawang trader and wanted a pastor too.

'Among them a fire has been kindled. A bush fire starts in one small area. Then it gradually spreads and increases in strength and fierceness. Finally completely out of control, it sweeps over miles and miles of bushland . . . the Gospel is spreading as rapidly among the Tagals . . . the progress of the fire seems almost out of control.'[1]

If it was not to be totally out of control and bring some of the strange excesses for which the Tagals were renowned, teaching was vital. At first, in addition to regular teaching as at Meligan, the Tagal deacons went to Lun Bawang deacons' schools. But in 1956 the first one-month Tagal school was held at Meligan and this became a yearly event. In 1959 it was held at the village of the Lun Bawang ex-deacon.

Towards the end of that school a special meeting was held. As a result 20 per cent of their number agreed to spend the first month of 1960 in preaching trips into areas where little had been heard of the Gospel but where there were urgent requests for teaching. This meant that some of the deacons would be giving more than two months either to learning or to passing on what they had learnt. What would happen to their farms? Members of their home

[1] *Jungle Fire*, S. P. Lees, p. 59.

churches agreed to care for the farms during their absence.

* * * * *

Meanwhile, a similar spontaneous expansion was taking place among the wandering Penan tribe of Sarawak.

The Penans lived in the deepest parts of the jungle, settling for a few weeks in little shelters made of saplings, leaf and bark, wherever there was wild sago and enough game. When that was gone, they moved on to the next area. Fearing that the sun would 'melt their brains' and equally fearing the spirits of the rivers, they never left the protection of the dense jungle, other than to appear for a trade gathering (*tamu*). Here they exchanged their jungle produce of resin for a cooking pot, a few beads, clothing and salt.

In appearance they somewhat resembled the tribes in whose territory they roamed. Like the Kelabits, Kenyas and Kayans, the men had pudding basin haircuts, though not usually as sprucely kept. Sometimes brass rings dangled from their ear lobes, though these extended lobes were also often filled with a large circle of light wood. There the resemblance ceased. The Penan was strangely pale, almost pasty white as he lived constantly in the shade of the primary jungle. His clothing consisted solely of a loin-cloth, several strings of beads round his neck and row upon row of black plaited grass rings worn below the knee. From this might dangle his diary or calendar, a piece of knotted rattan string, each knot representing a day. Their legs always bore the marks of leech bites, scratches and numerous scars from their endless stalking and hunting of wild game.

The Penans moved around the jungle in groups of from ten to forty and they were reported as being only a few thousand. They were mostly regarded as objects of ridicule by their more sophisticated and settled neighbours who sought to exploit them. As, however, the Kelabits, Kayans

Penan man

and Kenyas became Christians they began to have a concern for these despised nomadic people. A few months after an initial contact in 1951 with a group of Penans up the Silat river, a tributary of the Baram, it was reported that 'the Christian Kenyas were earnestly seeking their salvation'.

In the Apoh, the following year, it was reported that 'some of them are Christians, having been taught by the Kelabits . . . others are calling Kayan deacons and schoolboys to come and throw out their taboos and teach them of the Lord'.

As noiselessly and almost invisibly the Penans moved around the jungle, so the Gospel spread from one to another, no one knowing quite from where they had heard. They would just appear somewhere, sometime, for teaching, then disappear again for months.

A great step forward in the Penan work came in 1955 when a young Penan who had spent two years trying to adjust to school life with the Kenyas at Lio Matu, decided that God had called him into Bible school. The following year the Mission conference decided that it was time missionaries should start to learn their language and reduce it to writing. This was done at Lio Matu as it was a big trade centre for the Penans. Eleven Penans came from different groups for teaching, with a view to going back to their own groups to teach them. They sold jungle produce for their support, though this meant adjustments, as one of them testified:

'My people asked me why I didn't stay with them and have plenty of pig, but I wanted to learn more about the Lord, even though it meant often being hungry for meat.'

A greater problem was the sickness that came through the more settled life, and school was frequently interrupted. Over the next five months, though, reading primers were prepared and a little booklet of Scripture verses translated, and the Penans began to read. During this time also, other Penans came to the *tamu* not for trade, but for the opportunity of teaching. They drank in all they could before hunger drove them back to the jungle.

The missionary whom God called to care for and teach these wandering people was at first based in Kayan country at Long Bedian, upriver from Long Atip. One day she was interrupted. An old, deaf, Penan woman came and asked,

'What is this praying all about?'

As the missionary shouted the Gospel message into her ear, she opened her heart to the Lord. She was broken toothed, scraggy, itchy –she kept scratching her head with all ten of her fingers – and wore only the scantiest of 'bikinis', but Christ came to dwell in her heart and she went away with a real assurance of salvation, to 'tell the ones in the jungle about this'.

The Penans knew nothing of ordered life. The missionary observed that even sleep seemed somewhat foreign to them. They would sit up sometimes all night long around the fire, talking and eating. And they talked to one another about the 'Good News'.

In 1958 a school was started at Long Bedian. It was to be 'an informal preparatory school for Penans who are prospective students for the Bible School'.

'Forty Penans fresh from the jungle were learning to sing. They were all singing the same hymn but in forty different tunes,' were the opening remarks of the report on this 'school'. They studied the newly-translated Mark's Gospel, they learned to read and write, they learnt Malay and simple arithmetic. The report continues, 'They know now that it is actually possible to reckon the price of three baskets of jungle resin without using one's fingers, toes and the toes of one's neighbour.'

A little bit of calculation was very useful when the illipe nut season arrived. The illipe nut tree fruits only once in six or seven years. It is in great demand by chocolate manufacturers and so the school emptied when the time came to collect nuts. Four weeks later they returned, tired but happy. Great baskets of bamboo filled with the valuable nuts were lined up.

'This one's mine, these two are Geng's, that little one is Sigang's. She wasn't as strong as the rest of us.'

'And whose is this biggest one?'

'That's the Lord's portion that we set aside each week.'

'And this big one?'

'That's Nyipin's. He had an infected foot and couldn't get any, so we all gave him some.'

Out of the $400 they received from the trader, they averaged out $27.50 per head, with over $100 given away with great rejoicing. Penans were always careful to share out everything, but the Gospel had given them joy in much greater generosity.

* * * * *

To reach these people, the Gospel had spread along the normal lines of communication, just as among the Tagals – trade, finding work, visiting of relatives and casual meetings in the jungle all provided the bridges into new areas. It was the same as the Gospel moved south in Sarawak.

A Kenya man from the Upper Baram walked ten days to visit some relatives in the Balui river area. These people were pagans and he was Christian. He stirred their desire to follow Christianity and taught them a few Kenya hymns. Within a couple of years there was a small church of eleven families and a number of others interested. This was at Long Geng where the Cunninghams followed up the invitation to go and teach, and they found the best dialect in which to translate the Kenya New Testament.

Birds' nest soup formed a bridge for the Gospel in the Tatau river area inland from Belaga. A Kayan tribesman owned some birds' nest caves in the upper Tatau, three days' journey from his longhouse. As he collected the precious nests, he sometimes called on pagan longhouses, telling the little he knew of the Gospel. Soon SIB and BEM received a letter from some of the very small Beketen tribe asking for teaching. A team was sent and experienced a spiritual struggle as these rugged, well-tattooed, long-eared tribesmen battled to be free from the spirits.

'Let us not be hasty, let us say farewell to the spirits slowly,' was the advice of the witchdoctors, and the wavering continued.

'Put my name down first.' One of the witchdoctors finally rose to his feet. 'I want to become a Christian,' he added. The spell was broken and others followed.

Expansion was spontaneous, but the missionaries continued their work of both teaching and evangelism. In Dusun country they pressed out from Ranau to the east into the Labuk area. In the fifth division of Sarawak, visits had been made to the Limbang, and after twenty years, the work was reopened at Limpasong by a missionary couple. Missionaries had also gone to open a base in the mid-Baram at Long Lama, and missionaries and Kayans together went to respond to calls from the Bintulu areas.

In the Belaga area missionaries and pastors together opened up a work amongst the Sekapan and missionaries headed up the entry into the Pakan area. With these and other advances, it was estimated at the beginning of the sixties that the BEM's sphere of influence would extend to cover areas with an additional 100,000 people. And many of those were Ibans.

Fighting cocks

CHAPTER 13

WHY NOT THE IBAN?

'WHY did you look at that snake?' the Iban yelled. Labo Tadam, a Lun Bawang pastor, was helping a group of Iban people near Pakan with their farm. They had only just turned to Christianity and they wanted him with them, partly because they were still frightened of the old custom and partly because it meant he was helping towards his support. A snake had just disappeared into a hollow log. In their old custom, this snake was a messenger of the spirits and this empty log pictured a grave. Labo's action would mean that someone would die before harvest.

'Don't worry, I understand,' Labo replied. 'Our custom was like that. But we are not under the power of the spirits now.'

He prayed with them and they were comforted, but there was still a nagging fear. It was only fully dispelled when the harvest was safely gathered.

'Now I really know that your God is powerful,' said the owner of the farm. 'In our old custom I would never have lived to harvest our paddy.'

The Iban people near Pakan were very happy to have Labo and another Lun Bawang pastor living with them. A report from Pakan later in 1960 said that the two Lun Bawang pastors and their wives, in the six months that they had been there, 'had learnt Iban and endeared themselves to the hearts of the people under their care. They tell us of hundreds in the same area who are on the brink of becoming followers of the Lord. . . .'

Those hundreds did not become Christians and the work at Pakan struggled on with numerous missionaries and pastors coming and going to share in teaching this small group of Christians, and in outreach to the whole surrounding area.

In August 1965 another group of Ibans was contacted, this time in the Upper Niah river area south of Miri. Two Iban-speaking Lun Bawang pastors accompanied Mr Percy King, an OMF missionary sponsored by the BEM in 1963 to work among Chinese. He had heard about this group during his travels from Miri to visit the Chinese. This visit was followed up by other pastors and BEM missionaries, and in 1966 the group was reported as being ready to throw out their fetishes. The missionary member of the visiting team wrote at that time,

'We went from room to room searching, collecting it all, reading the Word and praying with them, singing hymns and instructing them in the power of the word and the Blood of Jesus. This took five solid hours. The pastor and I felt physically and spiritually spent. . . . We all met together to burn all their connections with devil worship. This was a significant time as they watched the flames destroying all that they had trusted in.'

The team moved on to other longhouses and when they returned to the first one, gloom and fear were over the house. The leader's little boy had been struck down with fever.

'What do we do now?' they asked, in the bewilderment of having destroyed the only way they knew to try to save this child.

The missionary, who had never before been faced with such a situation, found himself suggesting that they should pray, commenting later that it was a bigger test for him than for them. He prayed that God would reveal His power and love to these people in a way that they would understand, and to increase his own weak faith.

'As I finished praying,' he said, 'I was challenged to ask the Lord to raise him up before their eyes. For three minutes there was no movement. Suddenly he jumped up and ran to his mother – my soul just leapt for joy.'

It was not just Lun Bawang pastors who went to these scattered Iban groups. A big strapping Kenya man went to the Iban of the Bakong, a tributary of the Baram in its lower reaches. They were his tribe's headhunting enemies. They had become Christian after visits from missionaries and pastors, but he was nevertheless fearful. Who could tell whether something might cause a flare-up of the fierce tempers for which they were renowned? The pastor and his wife were received enthusiastically but living conditions were very difficult. They had to camp on the verandah of the longhouse with the dogs and famous fighting cocks as well as the fowls which came and went. Little teaching of hygiene had got through to this very new group of Christians and his wife made many trips to the river with washing in an attempt to keep their clothes and bedding clean.

The Iban were keen, but the meetings were anything but orderly. They wanted teaching for their children as well as nightly teaching for themselves. In fact they withheld the pastor's monthly allowance when he gave only four hours a day to the children, and would not pay it until he gave a full government school programme. But there was a response in the short time he was there and he left with the strong plea ringing in his ears, 'Please send us another pastor quickly.'

There was also renewed contact during the sixties with the Lubai Ibans who showed considerably more interest in the Gospel, but again their main interest was in education. 'Educate our young people. They will believe your message and become Christians. We are too old and set in our ways to change.'

The BEM was once again, after twenty years, being challenged by the Iban. There were pockets of response, isolated groups struggling to maintain their Christian way of life, surrounded by pagans. Often they were without any natural links with other SIB churches, and so far away that visits were infrequent. Lun Bawang, Kenyas, Kayans were seeking to reach out to their former headhunting enemies. And they were making little headway among the 300,000 strong tribe which constituted 30 per cent of the population of Sarawak according to the 1970 census. There was the memory of the rejection of the Gospel by the Limbang Iban and a feeling that they were different.

Obviously the greatest difference was numerical. The SIB had many churches amongst the large Dusun tribe in Sabah but in Sarawak, the churches were from the minority tribes. The Iban is the dominant tribal culture in Sarawak. Even the Chinese learn Iban in order to communicate with Iban, and so did the downriver Lun Bawang in the Limbang to communicate with the upriver Iban. But the structure of Iban society is different too.

Derek Freeman in his monograph on the Iban[1] describes them as 'untrammelled individualists, aggressive and proud in demeanour, lacking any taste for obeisance.' Although they lived in longhouses like many of the other tribal groups, Freeman also points out that 'the unbroken expanse of roof tends to conceal the fact that the Iban longhouse is fundamentally a series of . . . independent units of a competitive and egalitarian society'. The family room or *bilek* was the important unit, and it was quite common for one of these family units to move from one longhouse to another, provided there was some kinship link. Economically each room was autonomous, a factor which made it very difficult for a group of Iban to fit into the BEM/SIB pattern of supporting their own pastors, and the pastors in these Iban situations have often had very hard times.

Added to all this was the fact of the great strength of the

[1] *Report on the Iban*, Derek Freeman 1970. LSE Monographs on Social Anthropology No. 41.

Iban *adat* (custom). It seemed more all-pervading than in the other tribes. Where Christianity has brought the opportunity for progress to many areas, the Iban have been able to take modernization and education without losing the essential structure and values of the traditional society. Recently an Iban studying in an overseas university returned to perform the pagan ritual at his father's funeral.

*   *   *   *   *

The BEM and SIB were geared to an interior situation, whereas many of the Iban were living within reach of coastal towns and the new roads which were beginning to stretch across the country. During the sixties, the Mission was not only faced with these new challenges of the Iban. A small trickle, which would soon become a flood, of tribespeople was beginning to flow into these growing towns.

Secondary schools began to mushroom all over the country. In 1954 Hudson Southwell, who had usually been on the growing edge of the Mission's activity, had felt that he should resign from the BEM to be able to meet the new challenges of the younger, educated generation. He headed up a new community development project in Long Lama.[1] Here he was also able to minister to the spiritual needs of these young people who had moved out of their villages for further education. Although this was a parting of the ways in one sense, nevertheless co-operation remained close, especially as the BEM later began to move into these town situations.

In 1961, BEM couples began to minister to the young people in the new Miri Government secondary school. The authorities were 'anxious to see the young people influenced for good as they are very aware of the dangers

[1] For his success in this project which was 'largely due to his unbounded enthusiasm and his drive and energy', Hudson was awarded the OBE in 1963.

into which they [tribal students] fall when plunged into life on the coast'. Visits were also begun to the Limbang secondary school and in 1963, a school was opened in Marudi. Here the missionaries found Kayans, Kenyas, Kelabits – more than a third of the school eager to share in the meetings. When the Bario secondary school was opened on the Kelabit highlands, visits were made there too.

It was usually the pilots and their wives who were able to make these week-end visits which would not have been possible from Lawas without the quick and easy transport facilities offered by the aircraft. The visits were extras to already full programmes, as the BEM team was still stretched to the limit with ministering to the interior churches and pressing outwards to still untouched areas.

The biennial conference in July 1962 looked at the situation. Missionary representatives told of 'both advances and disappointments . . . from the Dusuns in the North to the Iban in the South. . . . A vital energetic church has emerged', but the Baram churches were 'shy and fearful' and in other places some exciting new advances had been followed by the development of nominalism in these churches. The report continues: 'The 1960 census figures for both Sarawak and Sabah show a remarkable increase in the number of Christians in the last decade . . . the increase is not due to foreign missionary evangelism, but indigenous propagation of the Gospel, resulting in "peoples' movements". This is God's method and God's time for these people. Such a work of God can be easily quenched, so tremendous responsibility rests upon the SIB and the BEM.'

Racha Umong gave a statement of priorities to the BEM at that conference which he enlarged when he visited Australia later that year.

'In our work there is one thing which is most important,

that is to preach the Gospel to those who have just begun to believe and those who are still pagan, and to translate God's word in each language. . . . Ask the Lord to give us the right type of missionary to go to Borneo, those who can translate His Word and who can teach the people. This is the work most essential in Borneo today.'

One month later, in December 1962, the Brunei rebellion erupted on the peaceful scene of Borneo and added great weight to those words. Change had come suddenly and unexpectedly. Next time it could be even more radical. Would the Church be ready? Had the Mission lagged behind in the handing over of responsibility as well as in the teaching and translation programme, so that the removal of the scaffolding would cause the building to totter? Temporary evacuation from Lawas of the Missionary and Bible School students and staff caused a considerable amount of rethinking for those involved. Things could never be quite the same again.

This was certainly true in the interior of the country where confrontation with Indonesia, which began very shortly after the rebellion, was bringing soldiers into previously isolated villages. New airstrips were built or old ones lengthened. Instead of the little mission plane (which during that time was severely restricted as to its movements) there were army helicopters landing and jet fighters patrolling the skies. But should there be other changes?

Lawas was the Headquarters of the SIB and the Bible School as well as being the Mission Headquarters and centre of the aircraft programme. Was it time consideration be given to a reduction of the missionary involvement at Lawas to give the SIB more opportunity to function independently? This suggestion was put to the missionaries, some of whom felt it was over-reaction and premature. The state of the church, which had been

163

causing such concern at the conference prior to the rebellion, was an indication that this was not a time for radical change.

Agreement was reached and the suggestion of the move dropped, but the disagreement caused underlying tension, and tension has spiritual repercussions.

When the 1964 Conference met, there was considerable disquiet. Alan Belcher, re-elected Chairman for a further two-year period, wrote: 'At our Field Conference in 1950 we were brought to consider our God-given task as finishable . . . now fourteen years later, we see a growing Church, the SIB, that has its own constitution, organization and ministry and which is financially independent of the BEM.' This was obviously great progress but Alan went on to ask how far the Mission had gone towards finishing the task. The answer is given in the Conference minute.

'In considering the future of the Mission . . . the goal of a mature Spirit-filled Church, essential to the completion of our God-given task, has not been achieved. We confess that this is due to our own failure to live in the fulness of the Spirit and we give thanks to God that He has shown us at this time our great spiritual need. We therefore look to him afresh to meet us so that His purposes in calling us to Borneo may be fully achieved.'

While praying for the renewal which God, in His own time, was to give in the seventies, the missionaries felt compelled not to get side-tracked from finishing the translation and training programme so vitally needed to equip the church to stand alone.

* * * * *

No one as yet could be spared for the new coastal challenges fulltime, but with increased education and literacy there seemed to be a wide-open door for correspondence courses, which would rapidly become attractive to those living in the towns. There were only 134 doing courses in 1964, as it was no more than an important side-line for a missionary with an already very full programme. But when a new recruit, Dr Bill Hawes, arrived that year, the situation changed.

Bill's call to Borneo was the result of the increasing interest in Borneo in the United Kingdom. John Smith, who had become the Honorary Secretary in 1957, followed Harold McCracken's example and ran the Mission's affairs from his own office in Reading, using at first his own secretaries for the typing. It was not until 1962 that Lesley Hobbs was appointed as full-time Office Secretary, and she continued to use the same modest accommodation. John did considerable travelling and speaking about Borneo in his 'spare' time, and the few British missionaries on the field began to be joined by a steady stream from the UK.

Bill was a doctor from London University. His principal burden, however, was for Bible teaching.

'During my medical course, I felt increasingly that I was being called, not primarily to medicine, but to Bible teaching. When I came into contact with BEM I found that they were a Bible-teaching Mission. There was Bible teaching at the Bible school, in the villages, and in building up the church of God in Borneo,' he said.

This emphasis was confirmed by the fact that just at the time that Bill was contacting the BEM, 'almost to the very week, they were praying that a doctor would arrive, whose primary call was to Bible teaching'. That seemed a strange request, but was accounted for by the particular way in which the BEM had developed its medical policy. BEM missionaries had always done a considerable amount of medical work wherever they went. Up to 1960 the missionaries were frequently the only ones available to give medical help, and all missionaries leaving Australia and New Zealand did a three-month tropical medicine course in Melbourne. Visits to churches, pioneering, running schools, even translating, all gave ample opportunities for medical help.

Even when a doctor had joined the Mission in 1952, he and the BEM had not felt that they should get involved in an institutional medical work, and the doctor had laid great emphasis on preventive medicine. Literacy materials were not only aimed to make people literate. In story form, reading primers gave valuable help to the missionaries in teaching hygiene and encouraging dietary changes. In some communities pernicious pagan taboos kept the health of the people at a low level and the freedom of the Gospel, together with teaching on food values, created dietary revolutions. The Mission showed the love of Christ by healing the sick and preventing disease, but as scaffolding to the building could not afford to be tied to an institutional programme. However, a healthy church has been a great witness to the side effects of the Gospel.

One missionary looked back over the years at the changes which had taken place. 'We taught them to wash their floors, to eat fruit and vegetables and to delouse their heads. Now when we visit them in their big, sturdy, clean longhouses with cement underneath and lawn back and front, we find the people clean, well-dressed, healthy. There are crowds of healthy and happy children.'

Bill Hawes arrived in May 1964 and was able to give time to the development of correspondence courses. By mid-1966 numbers had increased to 2,500. All of these were paying for their own courses and Bill was being helped by three full-time Borneans. The courses were a particular help in encouraging and building up the pastors in their lonely situations, but they were not the only ones to benefit. These steadily increasing numbers included students, police, field force, patients in hospital, prisoners as well as village people in the interior. The Christians were being built up but even pagans sometimes were being brought to study the Bible.

A missionary who was an enthusiastic distributor of these courses spoke of a visit to a pagan native chief's house. The owner was 'so obviously a native chief of the past, living in a house that was once the pride of the district. His wealth was seen not in transistor radios, tables, chairs, shining cutlery, but in rows and rows of gongs and beer jars and acres of very old rubber.' In the dark interior of the house, open jars with their bubbling rice beer 'added the usual nauseating aroma of rice beer to the general atmosphere of dirt, dogs, hens and distinctly grimy and aimless children'. But the eldest son had learnt to read and through this a shaft of light penetrated into this unlikely situation.

The missionary spent a couple of hours with this one man, showing him how he could study the Malay correspondence course. This man found to his surprise that he could actually answer the questions for himself as he compared the Malay with Mark's gospel in his own language. Previously his reading had been mostly mechanical and with very little understanding. 'The thrill and excitement written all over the face of the eldest son made the dirt, darkness and smell of rice beer seem unimportant,' the missionary added. This pagan man started studying the New Testament for himself.

Reading and books were becoming more important and the small bookroom begun in 1960 began to sell increasing numbers, not just of New Testaments and portions of Scripture but of good translated Christian literature. The increase in desire for literature stimulated several missionaries to start magazines in the tribal languages. The Kayan magazine ran for about nine years, and there were also magazines in Kenya, Penan and in Malay for the Bible school and pastors. The one with the widest circulation was in Dusun. In May 1963, the first 400 copies were distributed among approximately 45 villages. By 1965, the thousand mark had been reached.

'Now I understand what forgiveness really means,' said one subscriber. 'When it arrives, I read it right through. It takes me into the early hours of the morning. Sometimes the tears come to my eyes as I read it.'

The programme continued to snowball, the magazine making a major contribution towards the spiritual growth of many of the eleven to twelve thousand professing Dusun Christians in inaccessible villages throughout the country. Then in 1970, along with most other expatriates, the missionaries had to leave Sabah, but the magazine was taken over by Ibin Gillingan, former Principal of Nemaus Bible School and future leader of the SIB in Sabah.

* * * * *

Great changes had taken place in Borneo during the sixties and God was preparing Mission and Church for still further changes in the seventies. There was also a major change in the Mission, at the 1968 Field Conference. It began on 29th June, the International Day of Prayer when the BEM family worldwide was remembering the BEM and SIB in prayer. There had been certain frictions during the previous year. With apologies made and forgiveness sought and given, a considerable restoration of fellowship resulted among the members of the Mission team. Against this backcloth, God directed a change of leadership.

Harold McCracken, who was visiting Lawas for the Conference, reported on the change. 'On the second day of the Conference we were all deeply moved when Mr A. Belcher announced that he and Mrs Belcher had waited on the Lord the previous night and had been shown that he should not stand for the position of Field Chairman and that Mrs Belcher should not stand for the position of Principal of the Bible School. This was one of those dramatic moments which show clearly the Lord's leading. . . . The SIB representatives were visibly affected. They could think of no one other than their beloved *Meripa* (Alan's Lun Bawang name) to lead the Mission. It was only because of Mr Belcher's wise handling of the situation that they were able to accept such a tremendous change. . . . Their confidence in him enabled them to see that this was the will of God and to pledge their loyalty for the new leader.'

Bill Hawes was 32, the age of Alan Belcher when he took over from Hudson Southwell just twenty years before. Hudson had at that time been Field Leader for twenty years.

God had also clearly led Bill before the decision was made. John Smith who was at the Conference explained that 'his [Bill's] very evident calm equanimity amidst these historic happenings was explained three days later when he testified with deep humility that the Lord had spoken to him the previous Thursday regarding his future in the Mission'. Inevitably, as he moved into this new office, Bill looked back over the years with a view to looking forward to the possible changes which God would bring about in the unpredictable seventies.

PART 4

A NEW DAWN

1970–1978

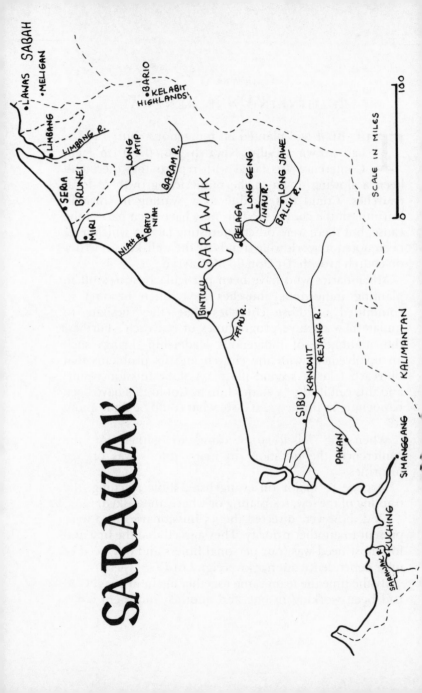

CHAPTER 14

RETHINKING AND RENEWAL

THE BEM had planted an indigenous church which had grown rapidly. Nevertheless, the 1970 Field Conference was faced with reports that there had been a slowing down in the numerical growth of local churches. Could this be due to a 'waning in spiritual warmth' of the churches? This may have been part of the cause, but there were other interesting factors which have been noted in worldwide trends by the well-known writer on church growth, Dr Donald McGavran.

Missionaries who have been particularly successful in planting indigenous churches have often become so committed to those churches that 'they hesitate to initiate new creative programmes of outreach'. Further, the attainment of indigenous leadership 'brings such an involvement with the church and its problems that outreach takes a second place'. A static mission results and this can lead to a static church. Could this have been happening in Borneo and if so, what could be done about it?

When the missionaries came to gather for the conference, the question on many minds was one of priorities.

'Are we to major on evangelism, Bible teaching, the training of the few, translating or what?' they asked.

God, however, directed the 35 missionaries who were present to another priority. They agreed that the first and foremost need was 'our personal fitness and our need of utter dependence upon a sovereign Lord'.

By the time the team came together again in 1972, God had been working in one and another and there was a deeper sense of fellowship and a further emphasis on prayer. This meant that the rethinking on priorities which had been forming in the minds of some of the Executive members during the two years, could be discussed and crystallized in an atmosphere of love, understanding and free discussion.

The result was the 'Twin Primary Tasks'. This stressed on the one hand continuing the Bible teaching and leadership training, together with the accompanying need for translation which had been of such urgent priority in the previous two decades. On the other hand, there was a new emphasis on the need for the mission to be involved in evangelistic outreach and church planting.

The Field secretary at the time, Colin Reasbeck, whose paper on Church growth had stimulated much thinking, discussed this in the Newsletter of August 1972.

'Are you surprised', he asked, 'that in 1972, the BEM should say that evangelistic outreach and church planting is one of its two primary aims? If so, then you probably suffer from three common misapprehensions about the Lord's work in East Malaysia.'

He went on to outline the three areas. Firstly, it was easy to think that the country had been evangelized. There had been such stirrings in the tribal people of the northern part of Sarawak and in Sabah, that it was easy to miss the fact that, at least in Sarawak, these were the minority tribes. They constituted only 5 per cent of Sarawak's population, or still only 10 per cent of Sarawak's indigenous people. The word 'Iban' for instance was still, in many people's thinking, synonymous with 'pagan'.

The second area of misapprehension was that circumstances did not allow evangelism to take place. Certainly there had been the system of zoning which had limited various groups to given areas, but that was no longer so. The result was that it had become possible to move into many new areas and Colin continued: 'Never has the country been more open . . . never has the country stood in greater need of evangelism . . . never has communication been so good.'

The third and perhaps most significant area needing to be rethought was the feeling that evangelism was solely the responsibility of the indigenous church. Colin pointed out that it had been exciting to see churches reaching out in evangelism, but over a number of years missions throughout the world had realized the effect of this emphasis upon them. The BEM was no exception to the trend. There was a dearth of what used to be called general missionaries, now more accurately described as church planters, whereas missionaries with technical qualifications were in fairly good supply. If these missionaries were mainly used in church assistance programmes of one kind or another, 'a paralysing effect can result and a static mission, denying its raison d'être of reaching out with the Gospel, can lead the churches it assists to become static too'.

As the Lord was showing the BEM the need to be significantly involved in evangelism once again, He was also giving a similar burden to the Bible school students and other members of the SIB. The SIB was eager to share in the evangelization of their country, and asked the BEM to ensure that the vision of the 'Twin Primary Tasks' should be implemented.

In the towns these two aims came side by side in a special way. There were the urgent needs to help and establish the young people coming into the towns from rural Christian backgrounds. But side by side with them were hundreds of young people coming from pagan and purely nominal Christian situations. They were English-speaking, educated, sophisticated.

'Our grandfathers were headhunters, and we go to University,' said a young Kayan as he set off for New Zealand.

In addition there were the townspeople themselves, particularly the Chinese, among whom there had not been a great deal of response. There were small groups in Lawas, Miri and Brunei meeting regularly and being ministered to by friends of the Mission.

Two missionaries, as well as Mr and Mrs Percy King, had moved to Kuching in 1969. One, seconded from the OMF, was a travelling secretary for the Nurses' Christian Fellowship and the other designated to work amongst SIB and other young people at the Teacher's Training College and in the hospitals. They were the first of a number of missionaries who would be stationed in coastal towns for pastoral work, student and nurses' work, Scripture Union, visits to hospitals and schools for RE lessons and great expansion in the field of literature.

The first BEM missionary couple to live in Miri moved there in 1972 and a few months later another couple and a single lady moved with a small group of English-speaking Bible college students from Lawas to establish the Miri Bible College. Hudson Southwell, who by now had moved to Miri as Principal of St Aidan's School, was able to give a few lectures in the college, and together they all shared the work amongst the young people. The BEM was beginning to plant churches in the coastal towns. These were small beginnings, but over the next few years the work greatly increased, partly as a result of the revival which started in the interior and moved to the towns.

* * * * *

In trying to date the beginning of the revival, one meets with considerable difficulty, as in trying to date any work of God. God is not limited by time and dates and the links in the chain and the many hidden factors can never all be discovered. The outpouring of God's Spirit on the SIB appeared to begin in Bario in 1973, but it is worth looking at a number of events which led up to those momentous days.

A missionary had lain one night under her mosquito net, listening to the buzz of conversation from the Kayans in the longhouse before they too went to bed. They talked of how wonderful the missionaries were. They talked of what wonders they could do with injections. They talked of how great it was to have the plane to visit them and to be able to have their really sick folk taken out to hospital. But there was no mention of God.

Of course the missionaries were praying already, but this led them to pray more earnestly. The area seemed so hard, but really they were only slowly coming to see the full implications of their initial turning to Christianity.

'I don't think our elderly people will ever really understand' was the despairing comment of one who had appreciated so much the concentrated teaching he had received in the early days of the little school at Long Atip. A few months later he was leading a service on the longhouse verandah. A tiny wizened old lady got up and shuffled to the front.

'I too want to repent of my sin,' she whispered to him. 'I have understood the message but I wasn't prepared to humble myself.'

There was a time of reaping and preparation for a further working of God's Spirit a few years later. God had been giving the missionary team encouragements like this in many different areas, but the times of reaping were sporadic. Then at the Field Conference in 1970 and over the following years God began to work in the missionary team. There are frequent mentions of an increased urgency in prayer for revival, both by the missionaries and members of the SIB. God had worked a number of times in special ways in the Bible school, and a report in April 1972 speaks of several students seeking permission to be absent from some lectures. Their reason was that 'the Word of

God was beginning to penetrate like a knife'. The senior student particularly had a burden to pray that he and the other graduating students would not only graduate academically but spiritually. He began to pray with a fellow student with whom he had experienced reconciliation.

The turning point came one night when the students spent almost the whole night in prayer and fellowship. There were periods of confession to one another and by early morning, prayer had turned to praise. The students began to experience a great new love for one another and a desire to share the good news with others. When it came to the vacation, they banded together into fifteen teams to go out and preach to their own villages instead of using the opportunity to earn some money.

'Can God provide for a man when he gives his earning vacation for preaching the Gospel?' was the question which tested the faith of many of them. But they returned to school the next term with stories of specific answers to prayer and rejoicing in the way the Lord had led and kept them.

A similar report came from the Nemaus Bible School a few months later. The one remaining missionary in Sabah, who was helping and advising the staff at the school, wrote of a 'very significant change' which had occurred in the previous months. 'Previously one could hear shouts and laughter for a while after every evening study period. Now, praying and singing are heard instead.'

The greatest prayer burden was for a renewal among the Dusun churches, and 'for the Lord to manifest His power for all to see'. In the meantime, God began to use the staff and students in bringing blessing to some of the Dusun churches. In early 1973 a report tells of at least eighty people coming to the Lord in some of the surrounding churches, and many more in other villages. Hundreds of dollars-worth of charms had been destroyed and even the very old had received new life. There again is the comment that 'there is a humbling and confession of sin' and 'many student teams going out'. The number of students seeking admission to the school had greatly increased and the churches were beginning to support the school financially in a new way. This report ends with the prayer that 'the Spirit's fire will keep burning'.

Change was also experienced in one of the new secondary schools in Marudi. 'I have a problem with my Quiet Time,' a student shared with one of the lady missionaries who was working there. Naturally she thought it was the problem of time or privacy or even lack of inclination. But not at all.

'All I want to do is spend time with the Lord to praise and thank Him. I always have a Quiet Time when I rise in the morning and I spend an hour or two each afternoon reading the Word. I read until the Lord speaks to me and then I pray about that. But this is having an effect on my school work. I can't concentrate. Is it wrong to be spending so much time with the Lord?'

They talked and prayed together, asking the Lord to bring order and discipline into his life. A week later he was rejoicing that God was helping him to give adequate time to the Lord and to his studies.

A few months later, in June 1972, the missionaries held a houseparty for the students and this led to a new emphasis on prayer. Two students began to pray every evening at 9.30 p.m. and gradually others joined them until there were too many for one group. They split into two. By December there were four groups of boys and two of girls all meeting to pray and study the Bible together. They were not only praying for their friends and members of their own tribes but for the many Iban and Chinese around them.

At the end of 1972, there was yet another great step forward in the chain of events. Dr Peterus Octavianus from the Indonesian Missionary Fellowship came to speak at the biennial conference of the SIB at Lawas. On the Monday morning, the 6.30 a.m. prayer meeting was hard and closed with prayer rebuking Satan, 'binding him and all his lying angels in the Name of the Lord Jesus'.

The next two messages were used by the Holy Spirit to convict many of sin, both old and young. Confession and counselling began and there were 'queues of men and women who waited until midnight and appeared again at 6 a.m.' Peterus always insisted that counselling should be done mainly by those on the spot and so Alan and Madge Belcher were involved in seeing many 'set free from the power of Satan'. Wrongs between couples were confessed, fetishes surrendered. Confession was made of sin – witchcraft, stealing, covetousness, adultery, receiving Satan's medicines. 'As cleansing and release were experienced through the Blood of Jesus, many exclaimed a heartfelt "Praise the Lord".'

News of God's working spread quickly and soon the conference sessions were being attended by many from the surrounding churches. For their benefit, Peterus requested interpretation into Lun Bawang and even this did not interrupt the blessing. His teaching was 'balanced and covered a wide area of spiritual truth and Christian doctrine'.

Peterus moved on to Sabah where hundreds assembled from far and near to hear him. Ibin Gillingen reported on the way God had tested them and rewarded their faith due to the uncertainty of Peterus' arrival. They had waited all day, much of the time being spent in prayer. Several pastors shared in teaching the people. At 7.30 p.m. they went again into the church and some of the people who had come from a long way away began to worry about their buffaloes and chickens. Ibin encouraged them to be patient, saying, 'If we are not patient in waiting for Peterus' coming, how can we be diligent in waiting for the coming of the Lord, the time of which we do not know?' Nobody went home. There was no grumbling.

Peterus eventually arrived and halfway through his first sermon, God began to work. Sins were confessed – some had grown cold, others weak, others had charms. One woman stood up crying and, in a loud voice, asked the Lord to give her the Holy Spirit. Many others 'received the Holy Spirit in a quiet manner'. Many stood for the first time, indicating that they wanted to witness for the Lord.

At the close of the meeting, Peterus offered prayer for healing and some with minor ailments were healed. Ibin himself testified to being healed of stomach trouble but added, 'We were aware that the Lord did not give big signs on this first visit, but He knows the circumstances of this country.'

From Ranau, Peterus went on to Mile 10 and God worked there too, and Ibin concluded his report by saying, 'Please pray with us that the Church in Sabah will have a spiritual awakening that will spread throughout the country.'

Peterus left Borneo, but on his way to Singapore he had to spend a short time waiting for the plane in Miri. While there he asked the Lord to open up the way for him to preach to that prosperous and vigorously expanding town.

It was just four months later that he was back again. This time he had been asked to speak at the four Easter Conventions during 1973. No one knew of his prayer, but he was also asked to speak in the Miri Church.

People came from everywhere. Kelabits and Sabans from the oil palm schemes, Iban from Batu Niah, Kenyas from timber camps, Chinese from Miri town, Lun Bawang and Kelabits from the Field Force and students from the Government sixth form college. In this sophisticated situation, the response to his appeal was immediate and spontaneous as many indicated their desire to know the freedom of Christ.

Peterus moved on to the conventions. At Long Atip there was reaping where others had sown. As early as 1970, God had worked at a young people's conference which the missionaries had been asked to run and this had become an annual event. God had also done a deepening work in the Baram when Dr G. D. James of the Asia Evangelistic Fellowship had been the speaker at the 1972 convention. At that time thirty people had dedicated themselves afresh to the Lord and these thirty had become very active in preaching, prayer, evangelistic trips to the Iban near Bintulu, to the Balui river and the Belaga area. Some of the young people had attended Bible courses and in 1972 the pastors had come back from the SIB conference really on fire for the Lord. Many nominal Christians and backsliders had been touched by the Lord. Sin had been confessed, many had been baptized and the half-empty churches had become full.

The people were therefore hungry and prepared to hear God's word as they met for this convention at Long Atip. 4,600 gathered and many families were housing forty to sixty extra people in their longhouse rooms. Some were getting up in the middle of the night to do the cooking, so that they would be able to hear the messages. Up to two hours before the meetings were due to start, people began making their way to the church which, as was usual for conventions, had been extended for the occasion. Many were touched by God and at one stage they were queueing up round the room which 'looked like a doctor's waiting room'. Two hundred were baptized before the convention was over.

Peterus did not preach an easy message. He was a 'hard-hitter with no time for frills or gimmicks'. He pointed out that revivals 'do not begin happily with everyone having a good time. They start with a broken and contrite heart'. The church's primary need was not, as one report put it, 'an upsurge of bright gatherings or an emotional binge, but repentance, confession and the forsaking of sin'.

Certainly God was working. Hundreds came to repentance, and counselling in each place went on into the small hours of the morning. There were healings too. They were not a major part of Peterus' ministry but he usually gave a fairly low-key opportunity at the end of a meeting for prayer for physical healing.

An influential Kayan man was attending the SIB Conference when Peterus suggested that anyone who wanted physical healing should put his hand on the affected part of his body, while Peterus prayed.

Taman Wan[1] put his hand on his heart. 'My heart was so full of sin,' he said later. Peterus did not pray immediately but explained a little further that it was not his prayers but God who would bring healing. While he did so, Taman Wan thought of his stomach trouble. He put his other hand on his stomach. But still Peterus did not pray. He wanted to make quite sure that they were trusting in God and not in the preacher. Then it was that Taman Wan remembered the skin trouble on his feet which had defied the skill of specialists.

'Lord, I cannot take my hand off my heart. It is so sinful. I cannot take my hand away from my stomach. Lord, you made me with two hands. Please remember my feet also.'

Peterus prayed and Taman Wan was completely healed. Such stories can be multiplied. Was this revival? Peterus himself did not think so.

'I believe that this is only the beginning of a spiritual awakening among you,' he said as he was leaving. And he was right.

---

[1] At the request of some of the church leaders, names of men and women in these last chapters have been altered so as not to bring undue attention to particular individuals.

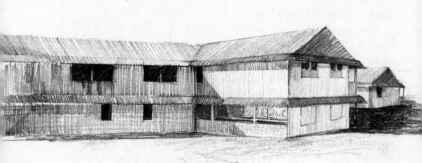

Ulong Palang

CHAPTER 15

REVIVAL

IT was a Monday morning in October 1973. Just an ordinary working Monday of an ordinary working week for the Junior Secondary School at Bario in the Kelabit Highlands. The only thing special about it was the very crucial third-year examinations looming over the heads of the students. If they did not pass, they could not go on to form four in the town secondary school.

Agan had invited his friend Galang to his room at the end of the L-shaped longhouse of Ulong Palang, so that they could revise together. Unknown to each other, both had been coming under a growing conviction of sin and on the Sunday each had given his heart to the Lord. They wanted to tell each other, but somehow found that they could not pluck up courage to do so. They suggested praying together. They each felt that perhaps they could let the other one know what had happened by their prayer.

Galang prayed first and while he prayed, Agan began to tremble and cry. He came under a further conviction of sin. Instead of praying about their exams, the two of them continued all morning in prayer concerning their own spiritual state. After lunch, they went out together into the rice fields where they continued to pray and the power of their prayer was such that a passer-by became hungry for the Lord as he heard them pray.

The boys returned home. Sina Balang, Agan's mother, wanted to ask them what was happening, but she didn't feel she could. The boys prayed again the next day and others began to join them. She was worried. They would never pass their exams if they went on like this. They were praying in English, so she had no idea what was happening.

'Oh, Lord,' she prayed, 'please make them pray in Kelabit, so that I can know whether it is good or bad.'

They were all praying aloud simultaneously as frequently happens in Borneo, but there is never any sense of confusion. Suddenly Sina Balang was amazed to hear her son's voice rising clearly above the rest.

'God has told me that we must pray in Kelabit,' he said in Kelabit. 'Then our parents will be able to understand.'

Agan's father was a teacher in the school and he too was becoming worried. When his sister-in-law heard what was going on and came over from her part of the longhouse to see what was happening, they all decided to ask for an explanation.

Instead of explaining, the boys began to pray. The sister-in-law was deeply moved and began to confess her sin. Sina Balang was pleased to hear this. She herself had confessed her sins when Peterus Octavianus was at the convention earlier in the year. Then she was suddenly taken aback when her son began to address her.

'Mother, you think you have no more sins to confess. But you have.'

Sina Balang, although her long ear lobes have been sewn up, still has the distinctive attractiveness of a Kelabit woman. She is ageing a little but the wrinkles at the corners of her eyes merely enhanced the sparkle on her face as she continued her story.

'I felt as if something sharp had touched me. I began to cry. Then I just had to go and put my arms round my sister and ask her for forgiveness for the grudge I had against her. It had never occurred to me that anything needed to be put right with her. After all, she was my sister. Oh, I was so happy,' she added, and her face was radiant as she recollected the joy of that moment four years before.

Her husband was still worried. Another teacher had

joined the boys but the church elders were still suspicious. They were working on the building of their new church right beside the boys' part of the longhouse. They had heard not only praying, but shouting and crying and it seemed to be getting out of control.

'Is it *ada' isung*?' they asked each other. In their experience such inexplicable behaviour could only be explained by the coming of an evil spirit on a witch doctor.

'Oh Lord, is it false or true,' Agan's father pleaded with God.

'I still don't really know,' he told the elders. 'But I know this. What is happening is bringing me closer to the Lord Jesus. It can't be an evil spirit.' He himself came to repentance and blessing shortly after this.

The movement spread to the whole school. One of the teachers confessed he did not feel able to lead their meeting. 'My heart is not right with the Lord', he said. A student asked if he could pray. As he started to confess his sin, all the others joined in and the service continued with much weeping, leading to shouting and singing of praise to God.

This was too much emotionalism for the headmaster. He was, not unnaturally, worried that school was being badly disrupted and there would be a heavy failure rate in the coming exams. He began to give heavy punishments of extra manual work to the students involved. To his surprise, they did it willingly. Then he too became the target for the boys' prayer. They asked to speak to him.

'Please, Sir, we would like to pray for you,' they said politely. The headmaster was angry. How dare they come to him like this! But, as he said later, he was somewhat puzzled because they were two very reserved and deferential boys who would not normally dare to address him unless he had first spoken to them.

'God, if this is anything to do with you, please send those boys back to me.' They came back a few minutes later.

The headmaster described the incident in a letter to a missionary a few weeks later.

'There are tremendous ways by which the Holy Spirit worked in us in this place since the beginning of this month. The High School Christian Fellowship was touched by Him first and then myself (the unbeliever, the wicked, the sinner greater than the greatest, the "Saul" who persecuted the Lord and was then forgiven by him). . . . These two children were used by the Holy Spirit so that I was forced to surrender to the Lord by the way they talked and prayed for me. . . .'

He threw away all his charms – except one. In a few days' time he had to take part as one of the main speakers in a very critical debate and he felt he needed just this one very powerful charm to help him to convince his opponents.

In those first few days of the revival, there was great emphasis on sin, particularly the keeping of charms, and on reconciliation. Sometimes those who had resisted God fell to the ground unconscious, sometimes for several hours. Then one by one they experienced wonderful joy and peace as they knew sins forgiven and new love for the Lord and for others. But still the elders of the church became more afraid that things were getting out of hand, as more and more unusual things happened. They felt the only wise thing to do was to stop what they could not understand or explain. They did not want to be guilty of allowing *ada' isung* on a massive scale. The young people were told they could not speak in the churches that Sunday.

The following Tuesday, Lian Matu, an elder statesman of the church, returned to Bario. He had been overseas and had several pressing calls for other things to be done on his way home, but he had felt an inner compulsion to return. He arrived just in time.

'As soon as I stepped out of the plane,' he related later, 'I could sense something new was happening.'

This was no doubt emphasized by the fact that one of the first people to speak to him was the headmaster. He apologized to him for the many times he had criticized this godly man.

Two groups of people came to see him. Firstly the church elders expressed their doubts and fears; then there was a group of mostly young people, who came and told him of this new experience which was filling them with such joy. In the next few days, Lian Matu attended the meetings in the secondary school. His presence there gave some of the older folk the courage to go along too, and many came to the Lord in repentance. Lives were changed.

One of these meetings was being held on the night of the headmaster's important meeting. He had to pass the school on his way, and he decided to drop in to see that everything was all right. Hardly had he stepped inside the room, when he heard one of his students speaking.

'There is someone here holding something evil in his hand. It is very powerful.' He tightened his grip on the charm in his pocket. They could not know about it. No one could see it. It was quite small. Someone else spoke up.

'There is someone very important in this room and he is holding something evil.' And then a few minutes later,

'He's a very important person in our school.'

The headmaster never reached his meeting that night. He stood before his own students and staff and confessed his reluctance to part with this most powerful of his charms.

'The greater amount of tears shed were on my own bed,' he wrote. 'All the sins were revealed to me one by one for at least four hours. I gave them all to the Lord wholeheartedly, then I began to feel so light and tremendously happy . . . I dreamt I met the Lord . . . I answered Him and said that I was sorry for my personal pride and again I cried in my dream. He showed me a book open to a fresh, clean, white page, where He wrote, "Yusup Jun Kalang was a great sinner but now has surrendered" . . . I was filled with joy, inexpressible joy . . .'

Lian Matu continues the story.

'I knew it was a genuine work of the Lord. Discipline in the school was no longer a problem. If someone found five cents, he would hand it over immediately. The very hard ones had been genuinely converted and I wanted the whole church to enjoy this experience. This is what we had been praying for for many years.'

After some time of tactful negotiating with the elders, it was agreed that another meeting should be held the following Sunday, October 14th, when they could study these events in the light of Scripture. Before that, however, Lian managed to arrange a prayer meeting in his own longhouse of Ulong Palang on the preceding Thursday.

'This was the real beginning of the revival on a big scale,' he explained.

Invitations were sent out to the surrounding houses and Lian himself led the meeting. At first it looked as if nothing was going to happen. He asked one and another if they would like to speak but they said that the Lord had not told them to. After singing several hymns, Lian suggested that they should pray again.

'Why do you seem so far away, Lord?' It was Agan praying. Then a few minutes later, 'Yes, Lord, you are here. You are very near. You are entering our hearts.'

With that about twenty people began to call out, crying in repentance and calling on God for forgiveness.

'It was so different from the sort of confessions we had heard in the past,' Lian continued. He let them carry on for about fifteen minutes, then, when they had quietened down, he said,

'I know you were repenting. But I am not sure whether you have really settled your salvation. I suggest you pray again. Confess every sin you can remember and ask forgiveness for them and for those you cannot remember. Ask for cleansing. Then ask God to fill your hearts with His Spirit. You can then be very sure He has answered. We don't want Satan coming in tomorrow or the next day, and filling your hearts with doubt.'

They prayed again, all speaking simultaneously. Then the Penghulu's voice could be heard. It was a very general prayer and rather impersonal. Just beside Lian was a group of school boys. They began to pray very quietly for the Penghulu, asking the Lord to help him to see his own sin. As he continued praying, his tone gradually changed and he began pleading with the Lord to forgive and cleanse him. With the Penghulu's heart changed, the floodgates of blessing were opened that night and continued through the Sunday meeting with most of the elders coming wholeheartedly to a new experience of the Lord.

On 7th November, Lian wrote a letter to friends in England, 'This is the most exciting letter I have ever written to anybody in my life. The Holy Spirit has come down on the Kelabit churches in the Bario Highlands in a mighty force somewhat similar to the story recorded in the Book of Acts, the Congo and the Indonesian revivals.

'The services are so different from what I have ever experienced before. When the Holy Spirit comes down upon the congregation, people begin to cry out in loud wailing (sometimes twenty and thirty people at the same time) calling out to God for forgiveness of sins and some calling the names of people with whom they have been quarrelling in a desperate desire to get reconciled. Many pending court cases have been cancelled because the parties involved have been reconciled in a very dramatic manner with tears and embraces of godly love. After the sin problems have been dealt with by the Lord and forgiveness granted, then the service goes on with loud singing of praises while tears of joy are still flowing down.'

Opposition was inevitable and showed itself very quickly.

'Satan is very angry and upset,' Lian continued. 'In Bario he has tried his usual weapons during a time of revival like this – heresy, division, spiritual pride and many others. . . . The new believers are very, very spiritually sensitive and Satan at times sends his messages and signs "from God".'

One of the women began swooning and revealing secret sins, and one and another had come to repentance. Others received 'messages' in their minds. But such gifts can be readily abused. One day a teacher whose speaking had led many to repentance received a 'message.'

'I made a mistake', he said to Lian in great distress. 'My speaking was not from the Lord.'

Lian saw the danger signals. They prayed and asked God to give them the gift of discernment. God gave the discernment that the devil was trying to destroy the faithful preaching of God's word. In many other ways God continued to use Lian Matu to teach and guide the young believers and to keep those touched by the revival on a firm Scriptural foundation.

October to December were months of dramatic happenings and great rejoicing on the Kelabit Highlands. The excitement of meetings and praising God was such that they might well have been tempted to stay and selfishly enjoy their new-found freedom of worship and singing of the new hymns and choruses which they were inspired to write. But no. They wanted to get out and share with their relatives and friends, and so they dispersed all over Sarawak as soon as the school holidays began, and the Lord continued His work. Preaching teams were organized in various directions in spite of the expense of travel. These were financed by a marvellous provision of the Lord when the school teachers received substantial arrears of payments that month.

The Penghulu, who found that there were hardly any court cases to investigate, joined with the headmaster and others in a long journey down the Baram river, preaching and teaching and seeing God confirm the Word by conviction, repentance, new joy and miracles.

The revival affected every aspect of life and the results remain to this day in a changed society.

'The oranges are still on the trees,' was how one Kelabit described what he saw in typical parabolic language. The children would no longer steal oranges.

But what had happened to the boys who should have been studying for their exams? The answer is found in Robert Lian Saging's BA thesis quoted earlier.

'The beginning of the revival caused a temporary disruption of classes in both the Secondary and Primary schools. This did not in any way impair the studies, for God blessed the students that year. The Bario Secondary School had one of the highest passing rates in the Sarawak Junior Examinations for form three. The school has since produced good results in spite of poor facilities.'

The blessing spread to other places. In the Apoh, it was once again among the young people where the hunger for revival started. They were having their ordinary week-night meeting. They had heard what had been happening at Bario and decided to plead with God to send His Spirit to them too.

The older folk were in the longhouse and could hear the singing in the church.

'Somehow the singing was different. There was something beautiful, sweet and real about it,' explained Taman Ngau, the translator of the Kayan New Testament.

The meeting seemed to be going on for a long time and the older folk went to sleep. In his sleep, Taman Ngau had a beautiful dream, so beautiful that he woke his wife and told her about it. He felt God must be saying something to him, so he suggested that they should read the New

Testament together. They turned to Acts, chapter two, where Peter speaks of the pouring out of the Spirit in the last days.

'This is it,' he exclaimed. 'This is what the Lord is doing. Let's go to the church.'

As they made their way down the notched log and across to the church, they became aware of people moving in the darkness. The whole village seemed to be going to the church.

'There in the church we found the Lord,' Taman Ngau continued. 'The whole place was full of the Spirit of the Lord. Young people were praying and worshipping. Some of them were confessing their sins and we began confessing too. We didn't realize we had sinned before, but we saw how filthy we were in the presence of a Holy God.'

Often two people would get up at the same time from distant positions in the church and go to meet each other. God had spoken to both simultaneously. They confessed their faults to one another and were reconciled. Even quite young children were confessing their own sin and then exhorting their parents. Taman Ngau's own little boy was weeping and he asked him why.

'Because the Lord died for me,' he said. 'He died for ME.'

As at Bario, one and another was given the gift of knowledge and secret sins would be revealed.

'You have not confessed all your sins,' someone said to one of the menfolk. 'You have a charm hidden out in your farm hut to make sure of a good crop.'

The man denied it, but the one with the gift of knowledge continued,

'You climb the notched log and in the doorpost on the left you will find a hole, and in that hole the charms are hidden.'

The deacons felt they should go and investigate. They

took the man to his farm hut – and found the charms. He repented and sought forgiveness.

In another area, where the church was lacking in well-taught leadership, such revelations were abused, or used by the devil to lead astray. One woman got up and 'prophesied'.

'God has shown me that we no longer need to read the Bible because He has given us His Spirit to speak directly to us.' The results in that village were excesses, divisions, and an eventual turning away from the Lord. However, such occurrences were not common, as God used Lian Matu to help men and women to be established in the new faith they had discovered. Over the following months he wrote many letters, almost Pauline in character, which meant that the revival went on, subject to the revealed Word of God.

The situation in Sabah was at first not so good. Division hit the group where God came in reviving power almost simultaneously with the work in Sarawak. A young teenage girl, who later went on to further training at Miri Bible College, was a Sunday School teacher when revival came to the village at Mile Ten. Kimbing, an experienced leader in the church, had shared with the teachers news of the Indonesian revival. He had suggested that they should pray for revival in their own village. This they had done for over a year.

Towards the end of 1973, when God was meeting the people at Bario, a Vacation Bible School was arranged at Mile Ten. They had sent invitations out to the surrounding villages and two hundred had come. As there were quite a number of small children, a separate meeting was arranged for them.

'I was in the teenage group on the second day', Kimbatoi explained while at MBC 'We were in the church and the small children were in a building nearby. We heard crying.

It was unusual crying so we all went to see what was happening.'

Kimbatoi noticed some of the naughtiest children of her Sunday School crying and praying. They were confessing their sins and asking for forgiveness. She was amazed and then she noticed her younger sister crying.

'What's the matter?' she asked.

Her sister looked up at her and, sobbing, asked for forgiveness for the times she had been disobedient.

'I was shaken,' Kimbatoi said. 'I thought of my own backslidden state. "Yes, of course I forgive you", was all I managed to say and then I too started to cry. I couldn't help it.'

She went on to describe how some of her friends had been telling her about certain manifestations of the Spirit which she had not been able to understand. She began to realize what they had meant when they started talking in strange tongues. Then she stood up to pray. One of her friends put her hand on her shoulder and started praying for her.

'I found myself talking in a language I didn't understand. I was thinking in one language, and yet my mouth was speaking in another one.'

Tongues were not a mark of the early days of the revival in Sarawak, and here at Mile Ten no one quite understood what was happening. There was confusion. Kimbatoi's father was a deacon and he decided to go away alone and pray and think. When he came back he was the first of the older people to recognize that this work was a work of God. But there were still some things about which he was not happy.

'This is of God,' he said. 'But not all of it.'

Naturally the young people felt that their gifts were being brought into question and they resented it. They felt that everything in the revival had to be of God. 'They were very dogmatic,' Kimbatoi explained. 'They wouldn't listen to Kimbing either. They even said he was resisting the revival.'

Sadly there was no one to whom both sides would listen, such as the elder statesman in Sarawak, who wrote in the SIB magazine a year or so later:

'In any revival there are usually two opposite reactions or attitudes of people including the Christians. Some people totally reject all that takes place, and miss out on the fresh blessings and deeper things of God, and even miss out on salvation completely. On the other hand, some people blindly accept everything without discerning, and are deceived by Satan or are misled by the flesh and are in danger of straying away from the truth. While we know it is the genuine work of the Holy Spirit, we must also remember that Satan is very active in time of revival doing his counterfeit work and trying to deceive. There is also the human element such as emotionalism and hypocrisy. Hence both types of people miss out on the blessings of God. We must recognize the genuine work of the Holy Spirit of God and the work of Satan and the flesh. We have to be Scriptural and well balanced. There are fresh blessings for all, even for those who consider themselves as mature Christians and spiritually sufficient and do not need revival. We should have positive and balanced response to revival in order to benefit.'

The division at Mile Ten lasted for about a year and a half. Kimbatoi herself took the side of her contemporaries until one day in 1975. They were having a prayer meeting. They were thinking about the exhortation to go and speak to someone with whom they had a quarrel before coming to speak with God. Kimbatoi felt uneasy. She had been feeling uneasy for some time. Kimbing was the one who had taught them. He was the one who had suggested that they should start praying for revival. It seemed wrong that they should be saying he was resisting the revival now it had come to them.

She began to realize the Lord was speaking to her. While they were all praying, she slipped out unnoticed and went to see Kimbing. She confessed her fault of criticism to him and asked his forgiveness. Then she returned and persuaded her friends that they too should seek his forgiveness. They all agreed that it was not right that they should be a divided people. God brought reconciliation, and gifts could be exercised within the context of a new love and understanding.

That was just before the Convention of 1975, at which a missionary had been asked to take the main talks. They were, however, not straight talks. Even with all those hundreds of people, mothers, fathers, grandparents and children, the hunger for the Word was such that all were ready and eager to study the Bible for themselves as he led them by asking questions. They soon discovered that they were finding out for themselves what the Bible had to say and what God was saying to them through it.

'The readiness to submit themselves to the Word was awesome', the missionary said afterwards.

As the convention drew to a close, one after another came to him and said, 'Thank you for the Word of God.'

CHAPTER 16

THE END OF THE BEGINNING

CHANGE is the essence of life in South-East Asia today. The SIB and BEM are no exception. Some of the changes which have taken place in the last few years have been directly due to the revival, some have been made possible by the revival. Others have been made necessary by the fast changes affecting the whole of South-East Asia.

The revival spread from the interior, from a village-orientated movement, to the rapidly expanding, fast-moving towns. Since the small beginnings of BEM involvement in Kuching in 1969, a church had gradually developed, mostly from amongst the tribal young people who had moved to the capital for training. One Sunday Lian Matu shared with this group what had happened in Bario a few months before. Closing the service, he walked to the back of the church with the pastor. No one moved. At the pastor's suggestion, Lian returned to the front. He suggested they should pray. When many began to cry, he remembered the noise there had been at some of the meetings in Bario, and felt concerned. There at Kuching the church did not have its own building, but met in the open area beneath the pastor's house in a residential area.

'Please do settle your problems with the Lord and confess your sins to Him,' Lian began, 'but remember there is a difference between here and Bario. Please remember our non-Christian neighbours and cry quietly.' Many that day got right with the Lord. It was the beginning of a significant work of the Holy Spirit in Kuching and from there the movement spread to other towns as the people moved from place to place. In fact, the deepening effect of the revival has remained strongest in the towns where there was more opportunity for Bible-based teaching, pointing the way to submitting exciting new experiences to the Word of God.

'I tried to remind them again and again not to be confined to experience but to study the Word,' Lian Matu recollected in 1977 as he looked back on the revival. 'There are some who were clearly used by the Lord who are now far away.'

Sadly, some of the young men who moved out of Bario for their further secondary education found that the sophisticated town life began to make inroads into their faith. They began to be ashamed of their deep emotional experiences in the revival. Further, they found themselves under the pressure of being known as 'the boys through whom the revival started'. They turned away, but wise friends and relatives have been helping them towards a balanced Christian faith.

This need for shepherding and studying of the Bible is stressed by an SIB leader's article in the magazine started in 1977 for the English-speaking members of the SIB. 'In revival it is important to advise the new babes in Christ to consult mature Christians, strictly to follow the Bible and not to rely too much on dreams, visions and promptings, although there is justification for dreams, visions and promptings in Scripture.'

This crucial factor of Bible teaching was also pointed out by Bill Hawes as he looked back on three years of revival. Explaining that opposition to the revival had taken the form of counterfeit gifts of the Spirit, counterfeit promptings of the Spirit and counterfeit dreams and visions, he added, 'Excesses have been seen when new life and enthusiasms have not been undergirded by a broad basis of biblical truth, and continued wherever there was no willingness to submit to the authority of Scripture.'

The SIB and BEM saw the need for renewed concentration on the 'undergirding of biblical truth', through the upgrading of leadership training and the spiritual education of the ordinary church member. The revival directly affected this programme, particularly in Kayan country. Prior to the Easter convention in 1974, the Long Bedian Bible school had been closed for several years, partly because it was poorly supported. As God worked at that gathering, the Kayans became very concerned for a local Bible school to train leaders for their church.

Not only were two thousand Malaysian dollars collected, half for evangelism and half for the Bible School which they proposed to build at Long Lama, but labour and materials were also offered. By May 1975, just one year later, the school was opened, having been built and mostly financed by the Baram churches, including the Kenyas and Penans. The staff consisted of one Kelabit couple, generously supported by the Malaysian Evangelistic Fellowship, a missionary supported by BEM and a Kayan to be supported by the Kayan church. In fact most of the money for this came from one influential Kayan whose generosity had been touched by the revival.

There was no difficulty in finding students for the Bible schools after the revival. In fact, both at Budok Aru and Nemaus numbers increased so rapidly that the staff soon faced problems. Numbers at both schools increased to nearly a hundred students, but some of these came in the first full flush of enthusiasm due to the revival, and then fell away. This even more emphasized the need for teaching and more careful screening. Both of these schools were fully staffed by the SIB and they needed help. A missionary was therefore set aside for in-service training of the staff with annual courses for all the teachers. Also there was on-the-spot supervision to upgrade teaching methods, and the teachers were given help with curriculum and with the production and presentation of lecture materials.

In May 1974 the Advanced Bible School was

commenced at Lawas for those who had completed their Bible training several years before and who had had at least two years of pastoral experience. Initially staffed by missionaries, the purpose of the school was to give additional training to selected pastors with a view to their training local church leaders in their areas. The staff sought to teach them how to study the Scriptures for themselves, how to find principles which could be applied to their own church situations, how to communicate the Gospel to various groups of people and how to plant and nurture churches.

Being older men, many of them brought large families with them into school and there were problems of support. It was for this reason that the intended two-year course was reduced to one. Some left their wives looking after their churches during the term, returning to pass on their new-found knowledge and abilities during the holidays. In these cases they were supported by their churches, but others had a hard struggle to see their way through the year.

'You know, it's wonderful how the Lord supplied our needs last year,' one of them testified. 'Nearly every Saturday I was able to get work and earn enough money to see us through the week.'

Instruction in the Advanced Bible School was in Malay and was mainly for the benefit of pastors and churches in the rural situations. Instruction in the English medium was given at the Miri Bible College which began in 1972. After a nine-month gap due to staffing difficulties, the College was reopened in 1975. Numbers were small but the calibre of students high. Initially the school was staffed by missionaries, but in 1978 Elisa Paul came onto the staff, after training at All Nations Christian College in England. In spite of Elisa's early protestations against any form of education, his wise father, Guru Paul, had persisted in encouraging his schooling and he was soon showing great promise. After being asked to stay on at his secondary school in Marudi as a teacher, God called him to Lawas Bible School and he was one of the six students to move to Miri with the English-speaking school in 1972.

During the next few years, three of that group went on to further Bible College training in Australia and other members of the SIB went to Indonesia and England. But the Miri Bible College is being upgraded to the standard of Bible Colleges overseas, which means that only those for higher study will need to go overseas in future.

While students moved to the various Bible schools and College for training, Theological Education by Extension was taking the training to the students. The English medium course was begun in Kuching but later this became an extension branch of MBC. Malay courses were begun in 1973 in Sabah, involving a total of 45 leaders. A work pass for a missionary to work for a limited period in Sabah greatly facilitated this development which continued until he had to return home in 1977.

Lay training schools in the rapidly-growing Belaga area of Sarawak grew from being held for two months a year during 1972–5 to being a full year course. A missionary couple were involved in this and they were able to share with the students in considerable visitation to the surrounding area.

Outreach and church planting continued to be a part of the training at all the other centres. Lawas had a problem here, being situated in the midst of the mainly Christian Lun Bawang area, but outreach teams to Limbang were arranged. From MBC teams went out in many directions, most notably to the Tubau Kayans, the Iban of the Bakong, and to the nearby oil palm scheme where a church has recently been opened.

The headman in the Tubau area had made it very clear twenty years previously that missionaries were not welcome. But he and his people had since visited Christian relatives over the mountains in the Belaga area. The MBC students who made five visits over a period of about eighteen months, suffered considerable culture shock. The students spoke the same language but they came from the Baram where their villages had been Christian for some twenty years. They were appalled by the living conditions and the extent to which the people were in bondage to charms, witch-doctors and other satanic influences. Their amazement led to thankfulness as they realized afresh the condition from which they and their people had been delivered. It was a new experience for these young men to be asked to burn fetishes and other paraphernalia including one protective charm valued at a thousand Malaysian dollars.

Even in some of these relatively undeveloped areas transistor radios and cassette recorders had penetrated and the church and mission took advantage of this advance of technology. Former missionaries in the Dusun field prepared a number of tapes for use in the scattered villages there and a missionary working in the Iban field from Batu Niah almost accidentally began a wide tape ministry to the Iban.

Amazed at the illiteracy she found in many of the Iban longhouses and faced with the difficulties of regular visits to so many small longhouses, she prepared a few tapes. The programme snowballed until there was a mailing list to over thirty different places. Not all went to illiterate Iban in longhouses. Some went to well-educated town dwellers, some to patients in hospitals, some to the Sarawak Centre for the Blind. Conditions were somewhat difficult at Batu Niah with sound-proofing provided by blankets pinned round the walls. But the church there took this on as a team responsibility, which outweighed the advantages of recording in the new tape studio at Lawas.

This studio was one of the projects of a group of 22 New

Zealanders who called themselves 'Men with a Mission'. Builders, tradesmen, farmers and tehnicians offered their services to the Church in Borneo for practical work. Their many jobs included two SIB churches, one in Marudi shared by the Chinese and tribal church, one at Lawas for the Chinese, the tape studio and other building at Lawas. It has been estimated that they must have saved the Mission and the SIB about three years of manual labour in the short time they were in Borneo. By February 1974 the SIB went on the air with thirty programmes in Malay, broadcast over FEBC.

While hundreds were learning from broadcasts and tapes, yet others were recognizing the new vistas opening up to them through literature. God called a young man to take over the supervision of Christian book sales. Converted through reading a Christian book, he found that books were his lifeline.

'I read and read and read as it was my only means of growth. I had no church to go to or Christian friend to turn to for guidance. Books ... were building me up, instructing me, shaping my Christian values and providing me with firm foundations for the Christian life.'

He began his own evangelistic campaign by distributing books. Now he is not only running the book room in Kuching, a town where sales have rocketed in the last few years, he is also responsible for overall supervision of the bookrooms in Sibu, Miri and Lawas.

This hunger for books was paralleled by hunger for the Word of God, again as a result of the revival. Reviewing the period 1973–1976, Bill Hawes observed that 'the revival itself has been the most significant factor in the development of the established churches during this period. The overall picture is one of hunger for the Word of God.' Translation was still a high priority.

Four New Testaments reached the people during the seventies: Kayan in 1970, followed by the 40 per cent

Kenya in 1972. The Dusun arrived in 1973 and the Penan in 1975. By 1977 the Kayan Old Testament had been completed by a team consisting of one missionary and ten Kayans who were supported by the Kayan church, two of them full time. There remains a considerable amount of checking which will be done by close liaison between the missionary who has had to return home, and the Kayans in the Apoh. The only Old Testament to be ready for the printers was in Lun Bawang, to which translation the Belchers had given top priority for the whole of the decade. There remain however many months of proof-reading before this book is in the hands of the Lun Bawang. In Tagal some books of the New Testament were revised and several Old Testament books were translated, whilst in Kenya, the New Testament was completed and two Kenya men were receiving training to start on the Old Testament.

*   *   *   *   *

The revival prepared the way for yet bigger changes. The role of the missionary was changing. During 1976, the Sarawak Government's 'localization programme' affected nineteen missionaries, either by non-extension of work passes or the transfer from professional to social passes of a number of the wives. The curtailment of expatriate activity which had been experienced for some years in Sabah now began to affect Sarawak, but at the same time there was a slight easing of the situation in Sabah. Two work permits were given.

God was not taken by surprise by these changes. 'Revival has prepared the churches for the departure of many missionary personnel. We sense too, God at work thrusting out SIB persons into former missionary positions. He is enabling others to receive valued training. . . . God's own localization programme has been planned well ahead of time. . . . What is happening is very painful . . . but we may encourage one another to be confident in the goodness and sovereignty of our God. He will look after His church. He will permit some missionaries to stay for a while longer to help the churches; others of us will be welcomed in other parts of South-East Asia to work with sister churches of the SIB.'[1]

SIB personnel were already beginning to contribute to these sister churches as they had begun to go outside East Malaysia to teach and to share with them the news of God's dealings with their country, as well as to learn from them.

BEM and SIB links with the rest of South-East Asia were strengthened by the merger between the BEM and the Overseas Missionary Fellowship in 1974. The seed thoughts for the merger had been sown some five years before but began to take more concrete form when the two Directors had discussions in England in 1973. Papers were prepared and the whole BEM and SIB fellowships were consulted. There was apprehension in many minds at first, but when the BEM met in Conference in March 1974 God had already been working further in the lives of the missionaries as they had shared something of the revival in the SIB. There was free and frank discussion, helped particularly by two representatives of the Australian and UK councils who testified that it was a time 'that would stand out in the memory of all present . . . as a time when the Spirit of God spoke to us'.

Despite the frank expression of divergent opinions, conference was 'remarkable for the sense of warm fellowship'. When the vote was taken, several members who had previously had reservations or been undecided, testified to the positive guidance which they had received for this move, though a few still remained hesitant. Continued positive attitudes after the conference were 'testimony to the way that the unity of the fellowship has been maintained'.

[1] Editorial to *BEM Newsletter* November 1976.

Because of the far-reaching nature of the merger, it was felt that a further conference should be held the following year. This was to confirm the constitutional and other changes which would have to take place, and to give an opportunity for Dr Michael Griffiths to attend.

There were other major changes at the 1974 Conference, demonstrating the changing role of the BEM missionaries. The flying programme, which for 28 years had so successfully served a church growing up mostly in the interior, was taken over by a Missionary Aviation Fellowship pilot who was seconded to the BEM. The gradual move away from a purely interior-orientated Mission was further emphasized by the decision to discuss with the SIB the implications of a move of BEM administration to Miri. The interior would not be neglected but the towns were urgent and important. The move was carried out in February 1975.

A natural sequence of this move was the suggestion to the SIB conference in 1976, that they should take over administration of the Lawas base. The ownership had been handed over to them many years before, but the Mission had remained financially responsible for the day-to-day running costs of such a large complex of Bible school buildings, offices, store rooms, bookroom, aircraft programme and latterly the tape and radio studio, as well as missionary accommodation. In order to help financially, the BEM began to rent the houses in which they were living and which had been built by the Mission over many years.

BEM missionaries began to take up key positions in the town situations where the SIB pastors were not yet qualified to serve. Their experienced men were not English-speaking. The Mission provided pastors for the Kuching church, the rapidly-growing Sibu church with supervision for several churches which began to spring up in the surrounding area, as well as the Miri church; a missionary couple also went to live in Limbang for a while. The church in Miri was dedicated in November 1974. The site, overlooking the town, had been given as far back as 1967 when a grant of land had been made for church buildings to BEM/SIB and the Miri Gospel Chapel. The Chinese church was developed first and their building was in use in 1972. Once the SIB building was completed, the numbers at both the Malay and English services noticeably increased.

In that same month, November 1974, the SIB in Sabah opened a church in Kota Kinabalu. Here there was no building involved. Some of the leaders of the SIB young people had been attending a monthly interdenominational prayer meeting and at one meeting they shared the need for a building for a church. A short time later, they were offered the use of the old Basel church, rent free. The Basel congregation of Chinese had moved to a new building. This old building also provided accommodation for the pastor, and the headquarters of the new SIB in Sabah.

The formation of the SIB Sabah in 1976 was reported as being 'one of those happy occasions when no disagreement causes division . . . the churches' relationship to the State Government alone makes it necessary but its results could well be a greater impetus for church growth'. Certainly it highlighted the significance of Sabah as a constituency. Half the churches in the SIB are in Sabah and one third of the total membership of SIB both in Sabah and Sarawak comes from the Dusun tribe. Over the decade the enforced exodus of missionaries from Sabah, together with the virtual closing of the border to Sarawakians wishing to reside there, had tended to isolate the SIB Sabah. At the close of the conference a document was signed by the two groups to the effect that 'though separate administrations were being established for the two states, there should always be a close bond of fellowship between the churches'. The two councils which meet periodically, remain closely linked in the sharing of responsibility for the Advanced Bible school, the aircraft programme, tape studio and Miri Bible College.

Many changes had come and there were churches established in Sabah and Sarawak, but what of the dominant Iban tribe in Sarawak? Entry into this tribe was being contested every inch of the way. In 1974, two missionary couples had been designated to Bintulu to establish a work among the Iban, interestingly the area in which the BEM might have started work in 1928. Gareth Littler travelled overland to Bintulu on Tuesday, 9th July 1974, and his wife Glenda was to follow the following day, by air from Miri. They had arranged to meet at the airport. That afternoon and evening, Gareth unpacked in preparation for settling into their new house in Bintulu which they would share with the friendly Chinese blacksmith and his family.

About 7.30 p.m. Gareth discovered a gas leak in the kitchen. The pipe to the fridge had come loose. He fixed it and relit the gas, not realizing that there was a great deal of gas in the small room. There was an immediate flash fire. Gareth rushed from the room and was taken to hospital within just a few minutes – the first car to pass the house was that of the local private doctor. But despite every effort of very willing medical teams in well-equipped coastal hospitals, Gareth went to be with the Lord on Sunday, 4th August. His young widow returned to have their first-born child, surrounded by the care of family and friends in England. God had given to Gareth and Glenda 'a specific burden for the evangelization of the Ibans'.

An equally strong burden was on the hearts of the Reasbecks who, in their turn, were forced out of the area by a serious medical problem for one of their small boys, which cleared completely once they were established in the work in Miri. And more recently a young Kayan in training had been visiting a group of Iban working on a land development scheme. They had built a church and were asking for teaching. One day, while the pastor was ministering to them, he received news that his wife had been taken to hospital. Next day she gave birth to a stillborn baby, and she herself lay between life and death for two days. This young man commented that he believed this was the sort of price that would have to be paid if the Iban were to be reached. Though severely tempted to pull out, he continued and other missionaries and pastors have moved into other Iban situations to take up the challenge.

The revival has, by and large, by-passed the Iban. In one area, where it appeared that similar blessing was coming to them as to the other tribes, there was no one with very much biblical knowledge to teach them. A layman who did his best to help them commented that he felt as if they were soldiers, 'ill-equipped and unarmed'. The revival was dissipated and the scar that was left caused dishonour to the Lord's name. What then of the future for the Iban?

* * * * *

On my visit to Borneo in 1977 I had the opportunity while in Kuching to join an Iban outreach team. This is representative of several in different towns and so I have again changed the names.

There were seven of us. Five went in Martin's new car and two on George's equally brand-new motor bike. Martin and George both knew that there were three and a half miles of very rough track between the macadamed highway and the village, but they were prepared for the effect on their vehicles.

Martin was an Iban who had been converted while studying at an overseas university. He was holding down a lucrative job. His new wife was Chinese, graduate of another overseas university. Then there was Anne, a highly qualified secretary and an Iban too. The other member of

the party going by car was a missionary who had recently switched from her fluency in Kayan to learn Iban in order to help with the outreach. She was in no sense the leader of the team. We were followed on his motorbike by George, a Bedayuh, and his Iban friend Kedu. George had come to the Lord through Kedu's witness and he in turn had become a Christian through the witness of a Lun Bawang friend.

As we drove along the dual carriageway from Kuching, a typical tropical downpour drenched the two cyclists.

'Cars have their advantages', we remarked, but the tables were soon turned.

'No road'. We stared unbelievingly at the signpost half a mile along the turning to the village. 'This road cannot be used until stones have been laid', and beyond it lay four hundred yards of two-foot-deep squelching mud. Now it was the motor cyclists' turn. Pushing the bike for that four hundred yards, they were able to ferry some of the party the three miles up the track, while the rest of us walked. Just as we rounded the last corner of the track, there was the little church perched on the top of a small hill near the longhouse. It was a simple structure of rounded posts, rough hewn boards, zinc roof. There was no furniture, just mats laid out on the rough screed floor.

Time was pressing as we had, of course, arrived late, but that did not stop the leisurely courtesies. There in the longhouse, timbers blackened with years of soot from the open fires, mats were laid out to cover the rather dilapidated bamboo floor. The guests sat and chatted. There was no question of the service until everyone had had a drink.

It was a happy party. These Iban had known the restrictions and fears of paganism and now they were starting a new life. They were building themselves new houses too and were beginning to collect some items of furniture. The bright red vinyl upholstered chairs in which we sat for our cup of tea in one of the family rooms later, looked very incongruous in the dingy, sooty cobweb-covered little room. One would have expected the city-dwelling visitors to look a little incongruous too, but they fitted in perfectly, with not the slightest sign of condescension or lack of ease.

Courtesies over, we moved off into the church as soon as was reasonably polite. Martin gave a simple and clear address and then followed the service of 'remembering Jesus'. The elements were a bowl of cooked rice and a glass of cheap red cordial.

A baptismal service followed. Martin had suggested the slightly unorthodox order of events in order to save time. No baptistry here – rather a muddy scramble down the steep hillside to an almost muddier pool – laundry, bathroom and baptistry – in spite of being so near to the capital city of Sarawak.

By now it was nearly dusk. It was cold and the mosquitoes were very active, but one by one the candidates went down into the muddy water, where Martin stood to receive them.

Most of the party scrambled back up the hill for a meal and another service in the longhouse before they could have a well-deserved rest, but Martin was preaching next day in Kuching. I returned with him and his wife the three miles to the car. As events would have it, it turned out to be three very rough miles. It was not only dark, and we had no torch, but after fifteen minutes a second tropical downpour made the going somewhat uncomfortable. But we could not grumble as God had held off the rain for the preceding ten days while they had conducted an evangelistic campaign in the Kuching church. They had urgently needed fine weather as the 'church', even though extended temporarily at the sides, was not big enough to hold all those who wanted to hear the Good News.

We eventually made it, muddy and soaked to the skin.

Martin and his wife returned to the comfort of their lovely home, a hot shower and cup of coffee. Martin then had to prepare for Sunday.

It had been a busy fortnight, with the evangelistic campaign, but weekends and public holidays were the only time when they could go to the Iban longhouses, because all the members of the team held down jobs which kept them very busy during the week.

Next day, in the totally different setting of the neat, clean Kuching 'church', Martin was again totally at ease and preached a sermon worthy of any large city church in the Christian world. God has not left either the Iban or the other tribes without leaders and gifted teachers. The new dawn has heralded a new and different day of opportunity.